JIMMY DOSS - OUTLAW

Runaway Boy To Outlaw Legend

DON RUSSELL

Order this book online at www.trafford.com
or email orders@trafford.com

Most Trafford titles are also available at major online book retailers.

Printed in the United States of America.

ISBN: 978-1-4269-5063-6 (sc)

Trafford rev. 03/10/2011

www.trafford.com

North America & international
toll-free: 1 888 232 4444 (USA & Canada)
phone: 250 383 6864 ♦ fax: 812 355 4082

CHAPTER ONE - JIMMY DOSS, OUTLAW

The steady rumble rolled from distant cloud-shrouded peaks. Deep, ominous noises that followed the storm created a mesmerizing feeling, a loneliness that caused a man's shoulders to shudder with the chill in the air over the high desert town of Silver City, New Mexico Territory.

A serpentine wisp of fog wound along the stand of cottonwoods at the edge of Elk Creek in the late morning hush. It was the kind of morning a man wanted to pull up a quilt and linger in the comfort of a fluffy-soft feather bed, not to wander out where the cool mist would reprimand a morning ambition.

In the mud-strewn main street, out front of the first adobe building at the edge of town, three sodden riders poked along on rain-slick horses. Wrinkled and weathered

1

hats were pulled down to rest atop weary eyebrows. The riders' hollow indolence disclosed they'd been on the trail throughout the storm. Their direction was fixed at the will of the horses.

From the distance no one could have seen the men's eyes ponderously cast side to side under hat brims, measuring the muddy street and pausing at each sign over doorways that came into view. They laggardly advanced into the rustic valley community that was an Apache campsite before becoming a settlement laid out near Chloride Flats in 1871, following discovery of high grade silver.

Murky broadcloth dusters engulfed each of the three like limp tortoise shells as they splashed through the puddles, shoulders lurching in tempo with each footfall of the horse. The younger one lifted his head; his eyes related a trace of confusion.

A large yellow dog left the boardwalk and yapped at them, side-stepping in keeping pace with the unpretentious threesome. They paid him no mind. The mutt retreated when one of the horses heeded his grievance barking with a twist of the head and a large, round, blinking eye. The wet matted-hair canine trotted back to the boards. He sat on his haunches and watched as if he'd done his part by recognizing that strangers had come to Silver City.

The desert bronze-faced man in his late twenties was uploading supplies in front of Mueller's Mercantile Store.

Water dripped methodically from the back of his hat as he looked up at the newcomers. Silently noting no acquaintance among them, he hitched up his chin in a lazy gesture of *welcome* without giving it any real thought. His presence represented the only other activity on the street, which was yet to come alive following the morning thunder storm.

The tallest man of the three rode an appaloosa; the spots on its haunch darkened by the rain. He pulled the glove from a hand with his teeth, pocketed it, and slipped the hand beneath the duster and lifted a thin cigar to his lips. With the same hand, he scratched a thumbnail across a match tip, cupped the hand and brought a red glow to the cigar's tip. An orange reflection of the flame showed against the wet whisker stubble of his cheek. He drew a deep breath, lifted his chin and blew a bucket-size puff of gray smoke that hung in the air.

"Over there, Squeek." The wide shouldered man clinched the cigar between his teeth and nodded toward the White Mustang Saloon. The three of them pulled rein to the hitch rail out front.

The shorter man of the trio, Squeek, slid from the saddle and threw back the flaps of the slicker, exposing a wide stubby neck and stout barrel-chest. A dark handled six-shooter was poked under the belt. His triangular face was coarse. The mouth and nose were pinched toward the center of his face, the lips in a pucker over two protruding teeth, giving his appearance similarity to a rodent.

3

Slats McClary, the tall man with wide shoulders, the apparent leader, threw a rake handle leg over the rump of the dapple-gray and set his long toed boot on the moist sandy soil. "Whiskey for the wet and weary," he spoke as if to himself. Bending stoop-shouldered, he focused on the batwing doors of the saloon while he snapped a rein over the slick pole.

The third man swung down slow like, an expression crossed his face that exposed a wondrous anticipation. He was young, not more than eighteen or nineteen. His light hair hung in snarled strings beneath the stained hat like wet, gold tassels beneath a surrey top. Thin marks of short whiskers pocked his cheeks and chin. He watched uneasily and followed the lead of the other two men.

The three of them ascended the double step to the walkway. Each turned their heads, first right, then left, noting the void of people on the bleached boards and the emptiness of the street. They paused at the saloon entry as if by instinct. Slats craned his neck over the louvered doors before slowly pushing inside. Still adorned in dripping, ruddy dusters, they sauntered to the bar. Squeek pulled wet gloves from stiff fingers.

"Whiskey...and leave the bottle," Slats instructed the barkeep in a slanderous tone, "we've got a little catchin' up to do."

"It's your poison, mister," the short-necked bartender yanked the cork and set the dark bottle next to the glasses he'd placed on the bar, "that'll be a dollar and six bits…in advance." The dubious faced bar-man wiped his hands on the stained apron that clung to his well-rounded middle. His lips flexed impatiently.

"Pay the man, Jimmy." Slats gave the young blond man an insolent glance over the cigar stub crunched between his teeth as he poured a glass of the sour mash for himself and one for Squeek before sitting the bottle back on the hardboard.

Jimmy Doss tossed the money on the bar; wrinkles in the corners of his eyes showed a hint of disgust with the tall, skinny man who'd given him the order to pay. He then drew a glass of the whiskey, held it to his chest and stared in the drink like a preacher at a baptism before hefting it to his lips and emptying the glass. A grimace grasped his face but his cheeks quickly shuttered it away.

"You boys got business here in town – or just ridin' through?" The bartender attempted conversation.

Slats McClary rested the hand holding the glass on the corner of the bar, slowly moved his eyes to meet the dark eyes of the inquisitive barkeep and drawled, "Yep."

The barkeep blinked, waited for more but Slats' answer was finished.

"We're just ridin' through…if it's any of your business." Squeek snatched the bottle from Jimmy's hand and sneered at the man on the other side of the countertop.

The strange threesome made their way to a distant table, scuffed chairs to the edge and unhurriedly assembled their heads in a knot. The skinny leader talked with a hushed tone while the other two listened and sipped rot-gut whiskey.

The bartender twisted a towel in glasses and took up conversation with two cowpokes that elbowed the shiny plank board in front of him. Time to time he'd look over their shoulders and try to give reason to himself as to the town newcomers at the distant table.

No words passed between the two clusters of men.

Within minutes the bottle clunked the three strangers' tabletop. In consumption of the whiskey conversation of the three ruffians had been low and secretly. There'd been no hint of a chuckle – not so much as a smile passed between them. The threesome emptied the bottle with a purpose.

"Let's get to it, boys." Slats rose, drew a deep breath and started toward the door. The two others followed his lead out the batwing doors and down the steps, slow and deliberate. Squeek adjusted the pistol in his waistband but no words were spoken.

The sour-mash was doing its' job. The three shoddy travelers pulled the reins free from the hitch in unison and walked their horses across the street and up a few doors to The Silver City Bank. They stopped and gazed at the black and gold lettering on the plate glass. An overhead sign swung inappreciably with the urging of a newfound breeze. The sky showed signs of pushing the storm over the darkened mountains to the north, but still, the morning street remained empty.

"Hold 'em, and stay ready like I told ya," Slats crabbed at Jimmy, "if there's any shootin', turn 'em head out," he hesitated, "but you don't mount up till after we do...ya got it?" With that the tall slender man tilted his head down and fixed his eyes hard on Jimmy's. He read them in gauging the depth of conviction he needed to see.

"I got it." Jimmy glared back, momentarily extinguishing the youth of his years.

With Squeek at his side and carrying saddlebags, Slats McClary ambled up the short flight of steps. The two men pushed through the door and quietly stepped into the bank and flailed open their rain slickers. Squeek contorted his face into a satanic anger, lifted the hog-leg from his belt and waived it at Wallace Higgins, the bank owner, and the two employees that donned white-sleeved shirts with dark green garters at the elbows. They all froze in place.

"Gentlemen, nobody has to be carried outta here by the undertaker! Just do as yer told and live to count yer coins another day." Slats had Russian .44's holstered at each side in full view for the bankers to see. "Now, open that there walk-in." He pushed through the short rail-door separating the lobby from Higgins' desk and the big vault.

The portly bank owner, attired in a brown pin-stripe suit and brocade vest stood at his desk. His broad-jowl face flushed crimson and the large pork-chop sideburns bounced in rhythm with the munching of his lips. "You can't mean that!" Wallace Higgins offered as a bewildered defense, not daring to attempt a substantial barrier that might endanger his life.

"Shor' as hell we mean it, old man…and do it quick like afore I crack yer head open and spill yer brains." The whiskey added confidence to Squeek's demand.

"I…I…don't know that I can remember the combination." Higgins pleaded.

Squeek was in front of him in a flash, "I bet a bullet in yer gut will git yer mind to workin'." The stout, mouse faced man cocked the hammer on his revolver and rammed the barrel into the banker's belly.

"Wait…wait, I'll do it." Higgins stammered. He dropped his chin to his chest and glared at the oppressive gunman before he took the half dozen steps to the vault.

CHAPTER TWO –
JIMMY DOSS, OUTLAW

Higgins wiped his brow and placed his hand on the vault's dial. He worked the combination awkwardly, pausing after each number set clicked into place. When it notched a final set, the bank owner stepped back and patted his shining forehead with a handkerchief extracted from a vest pocket.

Squeek again shoved the barrel of his gun into the ample midsection of the banker. Higgins grimaced with fear and anger as he spun the wheel to crank open the walk-in. He tugged at the enormous door with uncertainty.

"Git the vault money," Slats long thin face winced at Squeek, "I'll git the cash drawers."

The vile looking man anxiously pushed aside the flustered Higgins as he planted the .45 under his belt and

9

snatched up an oil lamp, flung the saddlebags over his arm and hurried into the reticent chamber.

"The three of you git to yer knees…over there," Slats motioned with the pistol. The bankers moved as instructed and dropped to the floor near Higgins' desk. The lanky outlaw crowded behind the tellers' cages and dug cash from the drawers, and stuffed it into a canvas bag.

A low whistle, blending with scraping sounds, came from within the vault. Squeek raked money and folded documents from shelves into saddlebags. "I do believe we's gonna be rich." The loathsome-faced man's voice was melodious.

Slats finished digging cash from the drawers and hastily stepped to the vault entrance. "Let's go…let's go!"

The two robbers staunchly moved to the front door of the bank. Squeek threw the hefty saddlebags over his shoulder and pulled the revolver, waiting for Slats to open the door. Slats holstered his gun and pushed the heavy oak door outward three or four inches, making sure Jimmy was okay with the horses.

BARROOOMM! An ear-splitting shot bellowed from inside the bank. The resonation of the blast rattled the structure's large front glass and unwittingly startled the outlaws. They jerked around, crouched and shook the ringing from their ears.

Higgins held a hand gun he'd drawn from a desk drawer. A small cloud of blue/gray smoke rushed toward the ceiling above him. But his unaccustomed hand badly misdirected the shot. The slug ripped into the door casing and rained down jagged splinters. He held the smoking revolver with both hands and pulled it to his chest, his eyes the size of silver dollars.

The rat-faced man snarled and cursed. He'd been humiliated into fear. He sprang upward…his face contorted, and he thumbed the hammer of his six-gun. Fire and smoke belched from the barrel. He kept firing, shouting and cursing, as he walked toward the three bankers. The gun clicked on empty chambers before it was over and the entire room overflowed with dark, rancid smoke.

The cloud lazily lifted upward, exposing Wallace Higgins and both of his employees lying in a jumbled heap; starched, white shirts oozing blood. A final gargle that flushed crimson-laced foam from the mouth of the last man to fall was the single sound from the tangle of bodies.

Squeek squashed his face and growled through his teeth as he thumbed cartridges into the smoking gun. "They got what they deserved."

"Let's git outta here…*now!*"

The two outlaws ran down the steps from the bank in a hunch-shouldered swagger.

Jimmy fervently turned the horses. He stumbled, and with a hand to the ground, caught himself. He grappled upright. Fear in his face was as distinct as a skunk on a dinner table.

Slats flew atop the dapple-gray with the moneybag in hand. As soon as he hit the saddle a Russian .44 was in the other hand. Squeek hopped a toe into the stirrup, the saddlebags still over a shoulder and he was astride the brown gelding in a flash. Jimmy Doss wrapped both hands around the saddle horn and swung up like a pony express rider with his horse already lunging up the muddy street after the others. He'd done as Slats told him…he didn't mount until after they did.

Maybe it was the whiskey, or lack of planning, but the escape route they chose required riding past the law office. Sheriff Matt Ragle and his deputy, Scoot Wilkins, heard the gun shots from the bank and were standing on the boardwalk in front of their office, revolvers in hand, watching the outlaws surge toward them.

Slats caught a glimpse of the lawmen. He yanked the spotted-gray to a skidding halt in the sludge. He didn't know his companions were close on his heels…but they were looking back toward the bank.

The three outlaws collided, long coats flailed and the horses screeched, stumbled and quick-stepped, somehow remaining upright. The bank robbers faltered and clung in

the saddles. Slats recoiled and pointed a .44; "Up there…
the law, up there!"

Sheriff Ragle and Deputy Wilkins confronted the
outlaws and fired.

A shot rang out from behind the bank robbers. The man
who'd been loading up at Mueller's Store when they rode
into town took a stance behind a canopy support post in
front of the store. His aim was good, but the crazed outlaw,
Squeek, was saved from taking the bullet when it struck the
saddlebag flung over his back.

The derelict outlaws, with guns in hand and whiskey
fogging their minds, had adversaries in front and behind,
either route out of town required dodging bullets. Slats
jumped his horse in the direction of the mercantile store. He
covered the twenty-five yards swiftly. The man was crouched
behind a water trough at the street's edge and ready to shoot;
his pistol at eye level and hammer back. Slats' .44 barked
three quick rounds at the man who'd first fired at Squeek.
His aim was true. The man jerked upward, yanked a hand
to his face – his hat flew backward. The slug crashed into
his skull over the right eye. He convulsed to the ground –
blood streamed between his fingers and one leg pumped
erratically. It was over. The angel of death took him.

Sheriff Ragle zeroed in on the outlaw that carried the
saddlebags. He figured the bank's money was there. A lead
slug twisted Squeek in the saddle; it struck him in the right

shoulder. A second bullet caught the rodent-faced man in the neck. He screamed. Blood spurted from the neck wound and he slumped, his head fell forward.

Jimmy Doss, the unpolished outlaw of the band, impulsively spurred his horse toward Squeek and flashed out a hand. The young thief yanked the saddlebags from the man who'd killed the bankers and drew the bags over his own forearm.

The stout-framed outlaw with unusual facial features was tough, even in death. He jerked the reins, the horse snorted, head held high – he twisted, hooves clawed the sky. Horse and rider tumbled backward in a brutal configuration. The gelding crushed the outlaw in the fall but the pain went unnoticed. Squeek was dead before he hit the ground. His horse flailed in the mud and fought free, righted itself and pranced up the street in a whimsical line that placed it between the lawmen and the two remaining bank robbers.

"Over there!" Slats shouted and pointed to an alleyway on the opposite side of the street. The tall, skinny man and tassel-haired youngster kicked their mounts around the corner of the buildings and into the alley, clear of bullets. Both men jabbed spurs and kept low.

When they cleared the last town structure and the shooting behind had stopped, Jimmy shouted, "Squeek caught one – he's a goner."

The rail thin man slowed and holstered the revolver. He studied Jimmy's arm with the saddlebags to verify what he thought he'd seen – that Jimmy had snatched the bulging leather cases filled with money. Satisfied, he shouted back, "Makes more for the two of us." He continued to slap boots into the muddy gray flanks of his horse as he led the way to the foothills.

Jimmy's mind raced. He shook his head, trying to see through the whiskey-blur and the frenzy that had just taken place. He recanted the look in Squeek's eyes when the lead slug tore through the side of his neck, recalled spurts of blood streaming from the wound and fear swept over him like a rabbit trying to outrun an eagle on the open prairie.

The fair-haired young man leaned far over the pommel and slapped his heels hard against the sides of the surging horse. The smell of the animal and wet leather filled his nostrils.

Keeping pace with Slats was mandatory. Running from the law and death were both new experiences for the young man from central Missouri.

CHAPTER THREE -
JIMMY DOSS, OUTLAW

Doc Jennings heard the gunshots that came from the bank. He rushed to the front window of the cramped two room office just in time to see Josh Darcy get shot. Josh was a younger brother of a good friend of Doc's and a young man of top quality, the kind of person Silver City needed in order to grow and prosper. Doc slammed the door behind him and with his black satchel in hand scurried toward the fallen man as quickly as his aged legs would allow.

"Let me through." Doc's voice was strained as he pushed the lawmen aside and knelt beside the silent, crumpled body. The anger that was aroused by the circumstances he'd just witnessed subsided and gave way to anguish. He extended his hand to the side of Josh Darcy's neck, knowing before he did so that he wouldn't feel a pulse. Doc slid his fingers from the man's neck and placed them on the eyelids – he lightly closed them to extinguish the cold, empty stare. The elderly, white whiskered gentleman poised on one knee and flexed his jaws in disgust that he wasn't able to do anything for the young man.

"Come quick, Doc!" Marsh Holstead held open the door of the Silver City Bank and waved imperiously for Doctor Jennings to hightail it to the bank. He shouted, "Looks like Higgins is still alive…hurry!"

The doctor was a small framed man, and at his age, not prone to cover much ground in a short time. He grabbed up the leather bag and after a stumbling effort to respond, moved toward the bank in short, rapid steps.

In route to the bank, the diminutive white-haired doctor paused impulsively at the body of Squeek, the bank robber killed by Sheriff Ragle. The .44 slug had passed clean through the neck and severed his spine. His head had twisted over his shoulder when the horse hammered him into the ground. He lay on his back with the full length duster gathered in wads at the midsection. There were muddy horseshoe prints on the duster and the side of the man's head. No need to check for a pulse; Doc sniffed, pursed his lips, nodded, and hurried on.

Marsh Holstead had separated the jumble of bankers, moving the two employees from atop Higgins' plump, blood-splattered form. The bank owner had taken a slug in the right side of his chest and another in the shoulder. He'd fallen first. As the outlaw advanced toward the three of them, his gun barking all the time, his aim improved as the distance narrowed. After Higgins went down the other men each caught lead in the heart. One was also hit in the throat. Their blood soaked bodies sprawled on top of Higgins.

Wallace Higgins was unconscious when four of the men hoisted his bulky frame to a desktop for Doc to make an examination. He cut the clothing away from the wounds and quickly packed cotton into the bullet holes. "Let's get him over to my office," Doc gave instruction, "he's lost a lot of blood…but I've got to get those chunks of lead out of him."

The town buzzed like a hornet's nest for an hour before things began to settle. Solemn, distraught faces meshed with anger on this darkened morning in Silver City. The people looked to Sheriff Ragle once Higgins had been cared for and the undertaker had done his duty.

Sheriff Ragle had become a top-notch lawman. The pride he held for Silver City and the town's people was evident in the way he handled the law duties he'd been elected to perform.

The early morning had slipped away. The townsfolk disassembled. They vacated the quieting street, their minds embellished with mixtures of anger and heavy clouds of sorrow, matching the darkened skies above their usually quiet and serene settlement.

Josh Darcy's body was placed in the wagon he'd brought to town for supplies. Ragle looked up from the dead man and said to his deputy, "Scoot, I'm heading out to Hank Darcy's place. Hank's my best friend, and I've got to be the one to tell him about his brother. Sorrow and desolation engulfed Matt but he knew he had to set that aside and stay shut of it. Matt had to take charge, like Hank would have done had he been in Matt's place.

The deputy, Scoot Wilkins, frowned, "He's gonna take this real hard…be as mad as hell too. You know he'll hunt them killers down and if he has to, he'll kill 'em."

Sheriff Ragle braced himself. Collected and confident now, he stood in front of the bank and began imparting instructions to Deputy Scoot. He emphasized the orders by extending fingers from a clinched fist a mere foot from the face of his deputy.

Stabbing the index finger upward, he started, "First, have Roland Grimes help you get some men together for a posse…seven or eight should be plenty." Matt held up two fingers, "Second see if you can find out who that man is," the sheriff pointed to Squeek's body. "Third, get a list, as best you can, of what was taken from the bank so's we know what we're looking for when we catch 'em, or if they stash the loot somewhere. And don't wait for me. I know Hank will want to ride with us. He and I will catch up with you and the posse. Now git to movin!"

Matt Ragle was a tough and hardy six feet even, stout shouldered and strong willed. The moustache added maturity to his twenty-six years and gave balance to the thick eyebrows over a firm set of hazel colored eyes. Folks had told him he looked like a lawman ought to look – he liked that, especially when he heard a fella tell it to Hank Darcy, the ex-Ranger who'd helped Matt so much in his earlier years, and been the inspiration for Matt to campaign for the law office in Silver City.

Josh's body was placed in the back of the wagon he'd been loading with supplies less than an hour earlier. They'd wrapped him in a blanket and placed him on a bed of straw before covering the dead man with a tarp. The sheriff tied his horse to the wagon back; the animal shied away, not liking the smell of blood. Matt stroked his muzzle, quieted him, and allowed time for the horse to get accustom to the odor. Looking up and down the street of *his* town, where he'd been the law for two years now, thanks to Hank Darcy, he put a toe on the wheel hub and stepped up.

Matt Ragle had known Hank Darcy from years back, having first met in Dumas, Texas. Hank was a Texas Ranger, having caught on with the Rangers a half dozen years after the War Between the States. The association between the two had started on a bitter note. Hank arrested Matt.

It was an hour before sunup when young Matt, then seventeen years old, broke into Haney's Store. He stole food and two carbines. The storeowner caught Matt as he was crawling out a back window. Haney held him at gunpoint and walked him over to the law office down the street. At the time young Matt was a cowpuncher for the Slash Eight outfit, having been run out of the house by his pa for taking up for his mother when the drunkard, Pa Ragle, put to whipping on her. A couple of months afterward Pa Ragle lit a shuck, leaving the family.

It had only been a week after Pa left when Ma Ragle came down sick.

She'd been sick for several days. Matt's younger sister rode out to the Slash Eight to get Matt to help – he was the oldest, and the girl had nowhere else to turn. Money was needed for food and doctoring for Ma Ragle. And the only way Matt could come up with enough cash, he figured, was steal some guns from the store; he could sell them to some of the other punchers out at the Slash Eight.

Once Hank Darcy found out why Matt robbed the store, he bailed the youngster out of jail and got old man Haney to drop charges. After that, on occasion, Hank took the boy with him on law work where substantial danger wasn't likely. Later, when the boy matured and learned to handle a gun, Hank would swear him in as a deputy. Hank was much more like an older brother to Matt during those days in Texas.

When Hank married Kate Farnsworth, he gave up the law work at her insistence and they moved to New Mexico Territory and took to ranching. Young Matt Ragle and Hank's brother, Josh went along with them.

The Darcy's homesteaded ten sections of land and built a herd of a thousand head of cattle over the next seven years. They'd named their spread Box D, built a nice log house, and six year old Tanner, their son, had a little sister named Becky, who'd just had her third birthday.

It was after noon when Matt made the turn in the trail that would take him over the rise from there he could see the Darcy's home. The house sat near the center of a wide stretch of ground that rose gently from the site where Matt tended the wagon, the body of Josh Darcy in the back.

The thin white string of smoke that curled skyward from the stone chimney gave notice that Kate was in the kitchen. He urged the wagon team forward.

From the window in the kitchen Kate saw the wagon top the rise. She went to the door and sighted the horse tied to the back. She knew Josh hadn't taken a saddled horse along with him when he'd left for Silver City. Kate held the corner of her apron in her left hand as she moved briskly from the front door, down the two steps and into the sunlight beyond the reaches of the overhang-roof. Her right hand shaded her eyes. Six year old Tanner ran and stood beside his mother, holding her arm, sensing her uneasiness. She bent, placed both hands on the boy's shoulders and held her face close to his. Within seconds, he scurried toward the barn. Matt couldn't hear the boy, but he knew Tanner must be yelling for his father.

- -

Slats and Jimmy had covered a good fifteen miles or more. They'd ridden fast and hard for a couple of hours, slowing only on occasion for the horses to catch their wind. They didn't dismount even then, staying in the saddle and turning often to look behind.

"Whatcha' think we got, Slats, five thousand or more?" Jimmy was anxious.

"I hope so. I'd hate to think Squeek went to hell for less than five thousand." Slats said it without much conviction, there was even a tinge of light-heartedness in his remark. Jimmy felt he'd be wiser not to say anything more, rather than say the wrong thing – he wasn't sure if Slats felt remorse about Squeek being killed, or if he was favorable, given the way he was talking and the comment he made about there being more for just the two of them.

Jimmy secured the saddlebags across the pommel, inside the horn. He could feel the considerable lumps. His imagination explored the holdings in the bags; '*could there be ten thousand…maybe eighteen or twenty thousand…what could he buy with that much money'.* But he also held negative thoughts; *'what if the law was to catch him…would he hang – be sent to prison'.* Their run from the law had taken them to the middle of the afternoon; the sun had come full strength. The two riders on the dodge were hot and tired. They paused in the shade of an outcropping, pulled the dusters off and stashed them under the bedrolls, back of their saddles. Slats packed the canvas bag that held money from the bank's cash drawers likewise.

Slats kept an eye on the boy…and the money, "You hang tight to them saddlebags, boy. We'll count it out come nightfall." He rubbed lather from the neck of the appaloosa and slapped it from his hand against his leg, "We'll get distance between us and any posse them folks back there put on our trail." He spat and tapped at one of the Russian .44's strapped to his side. "We'll not give 'em much to follow," the tall, skinny man focused on the saddlebags and gave Jimmy a sneering grin, "you just stay close, partner."

The terrain they'd covered was outlaw friendly, a lot of rock and very little soft ground to leave prints. Slats had dodged the law before. He knew, if there was a posse, they'd play hob looking for a trail to follow.

Jimmy had met up with Slats and Squeek a week ago in El Paso. The two of them had bilked a couple of drunken cowhands out of their month's wages in a poker game. Had the cow-punchers been open-eyed, they'd have seen what was going on. Squeek and Slats were bottom-dealing, slipping cards and laughing, having a good ole' time; Jimmy saw the set-up and went along. He was totin' beer to all four card players, making sure the punchers had plenty, distracting them while the two card sharks built their hands.

It was later that same evening that Squeek and Slats partnered-up with Jimmy, liking what they'd seen of the boy favoring their deception at the poker table. Two days afterward they told him they were planning something way bigger than a card game. He rode with them as a scheme was hatched on the trail between El Paso and Silver City.

CHAPTER FOUR - JIMMY DOSS, OUTLAW

Hank Darcy rounded the corner of the house with long, brisk strides. His manner indicated more than a little concern had been aroused when his son, Tanner, fetched him at Kate's instruction.

Kate anxiously moved to stand beside Hank when he settled in front of the front of the steps. She placed a hand to her forehead, shading the sun. Hank squinted into the sun under the brim of his hat. It was clear that the both of them were apprehensive as they watched the distant wagon approaching.

"That's our wagon alright…the one Josh took into town for supplies." Hank spoke quietly without turning to look at Kate. "And it looks like Matt Ragle is driving the team."

Kate gasped, "You don't suppose something has happened to Josh?" She dropped her hand and looked into Hank's face, uneasy desperation apparent in her expression.

"Hush now, don't get yourself worked up. Let's wait to see what's bringing Matt out this way with the wagon." Hank had been a lawman long enough to know there was serious trouble coming toward them, but he attempted to calm Kate. Hank dropped a hand to Tanner's shoulder, "Son, go in the house and see if your little sister needs some tendin' to."

The boy turned and shuffled to the shade of the roof overhang. He paused, not going inside, but stood by the door with a forlorn frown fixed on his face. A mixed feeling of fear and confusion welled up inside him as he looked from the wagon to his parents, and then back to the wagon.

The Darcys walked toward the gate and stood there, waiting for their friend, Sherriff Ragle to come closer. Kate raised both hands, drawn into fists, to her chin and looked into Hank's eyes…color left her face and her lips clinched. The wagon drew within ten yards before any words passed the lot of them. "It's bad news, Hank." Matt lifted his hat and tucked it to his chest as he dejectedly focused on Hank's face, a face that was rigid and hollow. "Josh has been shot. I'm afraid he's dead, Hank," Matt shifted her attention to Kate, "I brought him home." Matt turned and looked over his shoulder, indicating that Josh was in the back of the wagon.

"Oh, my God, no!" Kate raised her face full into the sun. Slight tassels of auburn hair brushed the sides of her face and tears began to swell and flow. Sobs came in near frantic gasps, her heart bleeding for both Josh, in his death, and for Hank, for she knew this would tear at him like a flooding river ripping through a settlement. The brothers were very close in recent years.

Hank's expression transformed from grief to anger, but he said nothing. He swung the gate open and motioned for Matt to move the wagon into the yard. The tall, handsome ex-Ranger pulled his hat from his head slowly as he looked down at the blanket covering Josh's body. Matt clicked the team through the gate, toward the house.

"Let's get him inside," Hank said as he reached for the corner of the blanket and pulled it back. The fatal wound in Josh's forehead had leaked a lot of blood down his face and neck. It had dried into cracked, dark crimson patterns that demanded quick removal so that no one would see him in such a subversive semblance. Josh had always been particular, demanding tidiness and cleanliness in his appearance. Both Hank and Kate knew Josh wouldn't allow himself to be seen in such discrediting condition.

Kate remained in the house with the two kids. She'd taken the bible from the shelf and sat in the wood rocker reading aloud with Tanner and Becky at her feet. She wasn't able to determine if the reading was to comfort the youngsters or her.

Hank and Matt went to the barn where they jointly began fashioning a coffin from wood left from building onto the house two years previously. As they worked the planks, Matt related the events of the bank robbery, being thorough and precise in detail. Hank listened solemnly, not asking many questions.

Hank Darcy was a tall, wide-shouldered man with thick coffee colored hair that coiled slightly over his forehead and ears. His eyes were the color of a twilight sky and they exalted the confidence and compassion of his physical mannerisms. The cleft in his chin added the strength of character exhibited in his high cheekbones and sturdy brow.

"You know I'm going to kill the man that shot Josh, don't you, Matt?" He drove another nail before he looked up, "That be a problem with you – you being the law in Silver City?" Hank stared into Matt's eyes, which were fixed on his own, but he saw no answer there.

Matt knew Hank wasn't one to make an empty statement. The fact that these words came more than a few hours after the ex-lawman's first knowledge of his brother's murder gave them credence. They'd not been spoken in haste, maybe in lingering anger, but Hank didn't say what he'd said in off-handed fashion.

Matt Ragle had given thought to the possibility that Hank would invalidate the law in his quest for retaliation. During the time he drove the wagon from town to the Box D and he hadn't set a decision firmly in his mind as to what he'd do. He figured he might have to decide on that some time or other, but for now he wasn't sure.

Matt didn't answer. The last thing he wanted was to get crossways with the man who'd done so much for him. But he also had to respect the badge, the badge that Hank Darcy himself had helped to pin on him, and the badge representing the law that Hank had insisted all men had to learn to respect. Without further conversation on the matter, the two of them went back to the final touches on the woodwork that was to be Josh's burial box.

The sun dropped low. It cast long shadows across the grassy knoll a hundred yards from the house. There, the wild flowers mixed with tall prairie grass that bent with the breeze, which was always present this time of day.

"Josh used to stand here under this sycamore tree," Kate said, as the wind gently disturbed her long auburn hair and hurried a tear across her cheek, "and always before he'd leave this place, he'd say, 'God sure know how to make the world beautiful'. It's only fitting this should be where he'd spend eternity." Tranquil tears filled her eyes as she stood between the two children. She held the bible in her hands and lifted it to her bosom; a prayer flowed softly from trembling lips.

The two men, with the help of six year old Tanner, filled the grave with the loose soil. They then placed stones evenly atop the grave as the hush of sunset beneath delicate, scattered, rose-colored clouds bade the day farewell. Hank marked the grave with a cross, having driven it into the ground with the handle of the spade. "This will have to do, Josh, until we get back."

The next morning, Matt Ragle and Hank Darcy rode into Silver City. They arrived with first light and the abrasive crowing of a rooster near the livery barn. Few words were spoken between them as they rode the dozen miles to town. Keeping their horses fresh, they gave them their head, not pushing. Not yet! The time would come.

Marsh Holstead, who'd discovered the bank owner still breathing the previous morning, stood in front of the sheriff's office with a steaming cup of coffee in hand, he knew they'd be coming early. The two men dismounted and after a brief exchange of words with Holstead, quickly went inside Matt's office. Holstead followed.

"Hank, I'm sorry 'bout your brother…it's a shame a young man like that has got to be killed by no-good coyotes like them that robbed the bank." Holstead waited for a lurid response of some sort, which didn't happen. He then tried to read Hank's expression, thinking maybe he'd learn something he could tell in conversation in the saloon later.

Mark Holstead was a man that liked to carry news. It didn't matter to him just how much of the information he conveyed was factual, and how much contrived. He had an affliction for being the one to *discover* or spread gossip. With another one or two people like him in town the size of Silver City there'd be no need for a newspaper.

"Thanks, Marsh, I appreciate your condolences." Hank was aware of Holstead's reputation and even though he needed help from him at this time, he disliked the man's character.

The ex-Texas Ranger wasn't a man to talk about what he thought or what he was planning. He'd seen men, a lot of them, who had more jabber than gall and he never found one of that kind he didn't feel a little cantankerous about. The West had attracted all types, but it had been Hank Darcy's experience that the men who talked first were the ones to take out when trouble came calling. The men with real sand didn't need to talk about things first...they just did what had to be done!

Marsh Holstead informed the lawmen that the posse had gotten away within three hours following the shooting. No information could be found about the dead outlaw except the bartender over at the White Mustang Saloon had heard the tall, skinny man call him 'Squeek' when they were in the saloon before the holdup. And the apparent leader of the threesome also had referred to the young stringy-blond headed man as 'Jimmy'.

"Squeek!" Matt Ragle scowled, "Doubt we'll find anything from a name like that."

Holstead went on - bent on telling anything he'd heard, "The man who seemed to be the leader was real tall and thin as a rail, probably somewhere around late thirties, and he rode a gray horse with black spots on his behind."

Matt Ragle added, hesitantly, as he disliked Holstead's exuberance and elaboration of meaningless detail, "The two outlaws that got away both rode horses with Texas style saddles. I'd say they took on the appearance of cowpunchers." He drew a deep breath and pressed his lips together in thought, "but the younger one, seems to me, didn't have seasoned riding experience of a bonafide cow wrangler."

More than half an hour passed; the free-talking man had spewed out just about everything that anyone in Silver City had told or had a suspicion about. He'd been saving considerable privileged information for his final commentary. Very few people in town knew just how much money the outlaws rode out with. The prattler leaned in closer, his eyes squinted toward the door and window as if needing to be sure the three of them were alone…"Over seventeen thousand dollars was taken, plus two or three thousand in gold." He squeezed his lips together and blinked slowly, feeling sure he'd impressed the lawmen with his ability to gather detailed information. Continuing in a secretive manner, the town gossip then related that a bullet from Josh Darcy's gun struck the saddlebags carried by the outlaw, the one that was killed before the bags were lifted by the younger man. Holstead leaned back, crossed his arms over his chest and stretched his neck, giving evidence that his dissertation was fully delivered. He measured the faces of Hank and Matt, looking for gratification.

"Good, Marsh." Hank nodded.

"Thanks, Marsh, you've been an enormous help," Sheriff Ragle was more convalescing in his expression of gratitude, trying to compensate a mite for Hank's brevity. The yack-jaw man had worn heavy on the two lawmen.

"When you're ready to take in after the posse, I'll ride with you for a couple of miles and show you the trail." Holstead again searched for responses, hoping for more than a simple answer.

"We appreciate it, Marsh, shore enough, we appreciate it," Matt quipped. He knew Hank had absorbed about all he could of the busy-body, "If you'll just point a direction, I'm sure we can set on their trail plenty easy enough."

CHAPTER FIVE -
JIMMY DOSS, OUTLAW

Slats and Jimmy rode hard and fast, in and out of cactus-laden arroyos, across rock flats, through stands of mesquite and needle strewn pine groves, staying clear of soft ground and sand. The wind that pushed away the storm supported their masking of the trail. When they reached the Gila River thirty miles northwest of Silver City they kept to the water, using it to bamboozle anyone intent on following, until finally, three to four miles upstream, exited onto a slab of shale that stepped up to a giant bed of scrabble.

More than once Slats considered doing away with Jimmy. He ran the thought through his mind, thinking Jimmy likely wouldn't be of use when he got to Globe and was to meet up with his cousin, Pete Murray. But then, the boy had shown signs of possibility. He did some thinkin' on his own back in El Paso, and when the lead was flyin' in Silver City the boy hadn't lit a shuck. He even saved the bank loot when Squeek took the hard one. The seasoned outlaw knew he could hoodwink the kid anytime…he was greener than a freshwater frog.

"When we stopping?" Jimmy was hungry, and as the fear dwindled he was getting tuckered. "Ain't we got enough distance – and with that river misgivin' anybody who was trying to follow us, I'm thinkin' there ain't a lawman alive who could keep to our trail."

Slats nodded, "Yep, I ain't seen no sign back of us." He figured they'd come better than forty miles. He glanced to the west, knowing the long shadows and desert breeze that sets in at twilight was also working against any posse. "We've given these horses some real what-for, so's I reckon we need to rest them good…be dark in a half hour, and not much moon tonight." He stretched his neck and looked ahead, "We'll settle up there under them cottonwoods. There'll be water and wood for a fire."

- -

The black gelding of Hank's twitched his ears forward, perking at a sound only the horse could hear. Hank held his arm out, signaling Matt to hold, "Something up ahead of us," he related in a hushed voice.

Matt Ragle prompted his field glasses and held steady, peering into the desert from the midst of boulders and scruffy fendlerbush. "Looks like Scoot and the posse," his voice trailed off, "and they seem to be heading this way."

Hank Darcy shifted in the saddle, looked to the distance where Matt had focused the glasses, and then back to Matt, "You don't reckon they're giving up, do you?" Anger was in his voice; his mouth grew taut and jaw muscles flexed as he studied the distant group of men.

The sheriff lowered the glasses, still looking toward the posse, "I'm not ready to say that, Hank, but even the posse's trail hasn't been easy for us, we've both seen how they split up several times to find sign – the men we're after have more savvy about masking their trail than some Indians…they're spankin' good at it."

Darcy was a determined man, one that once set his mind he'd see the job through. As a Texas Ranger, he'd hooked onto complex trails of outlaws and dogged them hundreds of miles. There was a time that he chased down a pair of stagecoach bandits from the Texas panhandle, trailed them to a dismal hotel in Denver, taking over a month to do so. He put a few grams of lead into each man's leg and toted them back to Texas. Another time the stubborn Ranger hunted down three long-time rustlers, followed them clear to Joplin, Missouri, and killed them all in a straight-up gunfight.

The name Ranger Hank Darcy was a name no man sideways of the law wanted to hear. He was as head strong as a hungry bear foraging for salmon in a mountain stream, and a crack shot too. The man could hit a silver dollar at two hundred yards with his Spencer and was known to put six shots from the Colt .44 in an ace of spades at forty yards. Not many men from Texas to Oregon could shoot as well, and only a handful could match his speed clearing leather.

Matt's deputy, Scoot Wilkins, with Roland Grimes at his side, led the posse from Silver City. They'd been persistent in tracking the bank robbers but without much luck. They'd separated many times, dismounting and searching for sign in heavy rock terrain.

"Useless as a hog in a horse race," Grimes bellowed as the posse pulled up, "it's like they's ghosts…just disappeared."

"Sorry, Matt," Scoot lifted his hat and mopped his forehead. "These men all got families, some's got business establishments, and besides, like Roland said, we never found a print after the river," he sniffed and scratched behind an ear. "They all voted."

"It's alright, Scoot," Hank said dryly.

"Most of them lost money in the bank robbery," Scoot went on, "and didn't think it was sensible to lose more by leaving things behind to fall apart."

A moment of quiet ensued, only the squeak of saddle leather could be heard as all eyes measured the dark-haired, strong-willed man, Hank Darcy. Every man of the group knew Darcy would push on, nothing short of his own death could stop him,

Hank sat his saddle, his face reflective of the hard truth; he knew the townsfolk were ill-suited for the job he must perform. The role of justice, searching out of the evil-doers, wasn't for shop-keepers or others of simple, unobtrusive life styles. The posse had served the purpose of satisfying themselves of a duty toward law and order in their town. They had displayed such, but their backbone jellied when callous hardships trumped the lax commitment within them.

Sheriff Matt Ragle's eyes quickly searched the grim, remorseful faces of each posse member. He then stood in the stirrups and spoke resolutely, "Thanks, men, I realize you wanted to help and we appreciate what you done." He looked at Hank and then back at the group of men, "Me and Hank will take it from here…you all can get back to your folks and watch after the town."

Scoot apologized again, "I'm sorry, Matt, but it wasn't going to do for me to go on alone. I'm not much at trackin' and if I was to get lucky enough to pick up their trail, I figured they'd see me before I'd see them. I didn't want to catch a bullet in my head like Josh did." Realizing what he'd said, he jerked his look over to Hank, "Sorry, Hank, I shouldn't have let my mouth run like that."

"It's alright, Scoot." Hank raised a gloved hand toward the others, "I'm going on – with or without any of you. Your help is appreciated. I'm not askin' for anyone of you to come along. Sure as hell, there's going to be shooting," he hesitated and glanced at Scoot, "and I don't want none of you killed on my account." In his gut, Hank had felt the dejection and disappointment in town people many times over when he was a Ranger. If more men, good, decent men, would place more emphasis to law and order, the derelict elements of the frontier would diffuse more rapidly.

"I'm with you, Hank." Matt swung his horse to stand alongside the stalwart man with dark hair jutting from beneath his hat brim.

The other men of the posse glanced at one another; a burden of disgrace gripped them. But through the apologies and sour admonition, they stood firm in their decision to go back to Silver City…except for Scoot Wilkins, "Being as how I'm a deputy, I feel responsible." Scoot's words came as though forced, "and Josh Darcy and those men in the bank were friends of mine."

"Not afraid to catch a bullet in the head?" Hank reminded Scoot of the words he spoke earlier.

"With the two of you along…I'm plenty okay."

"You know we'd like to go…wouldn't we men?" Roland Grimes spoke up and swung his head, a slight nod indicating each man, but he then quickly added, "But it wouldn't be wise for all of us to leave the town unguarded…could be those two killers led us out here then doubled back to rob the rest of the town."

"You're right, Roland," Hank was punching the ticket for the formidable lot of them, "you men best hurry, the women folk could be needin' you right bad by now."

Hank Darcy, Matt and Scoot sat with hands on the saddle horns as the disconsolate half dozen men started off. The three lawmen watched as the yellow trail dust amid rock formations and spindly Joshua cactus took the town posse from view.

Ex-Ranger Darcy stepped down. Lifting his canteen, he drank slowly; he was more in thought than he was thirsty. "Those bastard killers dawdled around the river for no other reason than to confuse whoever might follow after them." He pushed his hat back and checked the sun, "Their direction has been constant toward northwest…they know where they're headed…they ain't just riding to get shut of Silver City." He spoke with a reserved quiet, letting his thoughts flow unintentionally, "There's a small settlement called Buckhorn up that way," Hank pointed toward a pass through the mountains bearing west by northwest, "then there's Safford…and higher up that-a-way is Globe."

- -

Jimmy snapped small twigs, gathered a couple of hands full of dry grass and had a flame going enough to build on.

41

Don Russell

Slats pulled the rawhides from his trail pack and readied a coffee pot. Soon the two men had put aside the angry wolf in their bellies with hardtack, jerky and black coffee. Jimmy tried to hold back, but the uneasy jitters were as noticeable as a hog in church,

"We ain't seen nobody on our trail, you figure no one came after us?" Jimmie Doss rubbed his hand together, staring into the fire and then at the skinny man.

"Can't never be sure. I got me a strange feeling inside." Slats chewed on a stem of bunch grass and glared toward Jimmy with unfocused eyes, like he could see a whole clean through him, "Sometimes a hard-headed lawman will dog a man worse than a hungry Comanche on the trail of a wounded antelope." He threw sticks of mesquite on the fire, seeming to Jimmy he defied the possibility of fear that someone would see the light.

"Maybe we shouldn't have stopped at that saloon in Safford." Jimmy's words were spoken like half question – half fact.

"I ain't afraid of no suicide-seekin' lawman. Slats spat the piece of grass from his mouth and wiped a backhand across his lips, picked up an amber bottle and jerked the cork, "Besides, if we hadn't gone in there we couldn't have no whiskey now." He lifted the bottle and took two long pulls.

Jimmy rifled his hands through his hair and shook both hands vigorously with fingers embedded in the heavy tresses of dirty blond tangles.

"We gonna count it now?" The words came out faster than he'd planned.

Slats cheeked a wry grin, "Thought we'd wait till morning."

The boy's eyes grew dark…then he saw the distorted smile, "Ah, yer funnin' me!" Jimmy smiled and scooted closer to Slats and the fire, the saddlebags already pushed in front of him. Little did he know, but the skinny, hollow-cheeked man had already slipped two large stacks of bills out of the saddlebags and into his rifle boot while Jimmy gathered firewood and water.

A saddle blanket served as a tabletop. Slats slowly drew bundles of bills from the bags, all the while watching the pie-eyed-boy-outlaw meditate in the glory of becoming rich. The big man then spread the gold coins atop the paper money like he was adding gravy to a plate of fresh cooked steak and potatoes.

"Gosh, almighty, I didn't know there was that much money in the world," Jimmy's grin swelled, "I'm gonna live like a king."

Slats counted out two piles of bills, each with four thousand dollars – one more band of currency was to be counted, and the nearly two pounds of gold coins were yet to be divided.

The young man's eyes fixed on the money in front of him, "Maybe we can get in a poker game; I ain't never had money like this to gamble." His eyes widened, "With a stack like this I bet I can buy me some bluff hands."

"Boy, this is only the beginning." He gathered up his share of the loot in his long toothpick fingers and stuffed it into the canvas bag and then everything went back into the saddlebags except for a roll of bills he stashed in a jeans pocket. He handed Jimmy a small roll of cash, "Here's a couple hundred for now," Slats buckled back the leather straps and pulled the saddlebags to his midsection, "you'll get your full share when we get to where we're goin'."

"And where that might be, partner?"

"We're headin' on up to Globe…that's Arizona Territory, I got me a cousin up there what knows how to get some real money."

"Yea, like this ain't real money." Jimmy's bear-in-the-honey-pot grin diminished, melting like a snow bank on a July afternoon, when he looked up at Slats. The lanky outlaw had stood to full height and held a Russian .44 loosely in the fingers of his right hand. The hair on the back of the young man's neck bristled. Slats rolled the cylinder and slipped the gun into the tie-down holster, "I make it a habit to make sure my killin'-iron is ready before I turn in…a man never knows when he might have to up and shoot before both eyes come open."

"Yea," Jimmy Doss said as he blew away the air he'd just gasped into his lungs a moment before, "a man never knows." Then and there Jimmy learned a lesson in staying alive. Trust shouldn't being taken too lightly. He lay back against the warm leather of his saddle, his head cocked forward, and starred into the fire, thinking about the bank robbery, Squeek getting killed, and the long run he and Slats had made. Sleep finally came…he was tired to the bone.

CHAPTER SIX –
JIMMY DOSS, OUTLAW

The tall Irishman had been crossways of the law most of his life. As a boy in New York he'd been a torment for his parents, always in trouble. The cops could spot him in a gang of street hooligans because he was taller than the others. He suffered consequences even of others didn't.

When in his early twenties he twice served prison time, once in New York, the other in Ohio. During the States War years, he avoided military duty, and for the recent fifteen years he was on the dodge, ranging from Arkansas west through the states and territories clear to California. Three years ago he'd ridden the trail from west Texas through Silver City to Globe in Arizona Territory with his cousin, Pete. Back then Globe wasn't more than a tent town.

Slats studied the jagged mountains on either side as they rode. The stagecoach trail he and Jimmy followed was once an old Indian trading trace. Both the Navajo and their cousins, the Apaches, used it for hundreds of years before the coming of the whites.

The callous outlaw had watched the notched mountain tops for hours; he pulled the appaloosa to a halt, thumbed back his hat and lifted his chin, "Up that mountain…that's the shortcut, saves ten or twelve hours better'n the stage route.

"We gotta go up there?" Jimmy gawked upward and smirked at his outlaw partner.

Slats gave Jimmy a sneer, "You heard me," he continued to study the peaks… "and as I recall there's an old prospector what lives up thata' way, in the mountain valley – got himself a young wife. He was workin' the rocks up from the crick – maybe has some gold he'd want to share with us," Slats grunted.

"That don't look like no trail." Jimmy said back, "More like a rock-slide than a trail, if you ask me."

"Well, I didn't ask."

Both men lazily dropped from the saddles. "More scrabble rock there than was before…," Slats scratched his neck whiskers, "but I know this is it."

Jimmy wiped the sweat from his face with a forearm, and quiet-like he uttered, "Seems to me that ain't no trail no more." But he mounted up as Slats did and they made their way up a slope to a grove of skimpy aspens. They were soon caught up in rocks strewn amidst the remnants of a rockslide. Any choice of a route up the mountainside was to be plenty difficult, but not impossible.

More than an hour of hard effort passed. The bedraggled outlaws completed a strenuous, sun baked climb, rising almost twelve hundred feet. When they reached stable footing at the top, they wilted into a much needed rest. From where they stood, a game trail slanted into the cut at an angle and disappeared behind the rocks and squatty pines.

"All them slides weren't there the last time," Slats woofed. He looked ahead, "But this here was the trail." He pointed to a mountain valley of prairie grass with a creek meandering through, roughly a half mile ahead and three to four hundred feet below, "That valley there," he spoke slowly, catching his wind, "there's a cabin sits behind that brace of boulders where the stream parries out of sight from here."

"You sure?" Jimmy squinted to the direction Slats pointed.

"Boy, quit asking me if I'm sure." Slats' hollow cheeks flexed but he held his anger. "I'm sure enough that if you want to wager your share of the bank take, we'll just make that bet here and now."

The younger man overlooked the remark, "People living there?" Jimmy held his hat to shield the sun as he gaped at the area the slender man described.

Slats lit a slim cigar and blew smoke from the side of his mouth. "Last time I was here the man who was there, the one who was bent on striking a vein of gold was livin' there…with his woman and a boy. I reckon if he found gold they'll likely still be there…if not, probably they's gone."

The poorly matched pair of outlaws made their way down the steep slope, savoring the easy ride and looking forward to reaching the cabin Slats recounted. "I hope them people are home, I'm hungry enough to eat a live hog," Jimmy wafted between the creaks and leather-moans of the saddles.

"Yea, sounds good. When me and Pete came through, they dished us up some fine grub. That ol' boy there had him a fine cook in that woman… I'm thinkin' his name was Isaiah…Isaiah Worsham, I believe it was…him and his young squaw wife…and…"

"A squaw?" Jimmy blurted back.

"Yep…says he traded for her up in Wyoming country when she was about fourteen," Slats drew the words out, "her pap was a Shoshone chief and her ma a white woman – said she was taken from a wagon train headed for Oregon."

Jimmy's face wrinkled, "They got a family?"

"They had a boy…a little scamp then about four or five I suppose. But he was already trackin' and shootin' for table food."

The gritty-haired blond outlaw took in Slats' words, remembering his mother and his early childhood back in Missouri before his folks were killed.

The horses stopped at the stream's edge. The water sparkled. Sunlight reflected brilliant flashes that twinkled like stars, bouncing inconsistently. The men and their horses drank their fill, all the while keeping an eye toward the cabin that sat a good distance ahead of a sweeping bend in the burbling rock-bed stream. A fresh new curl of smoke rose from the chimney,

"Someone's home," a wide grin came to the young man's face.

They walked their horses along the tall grass that bordered the creek and fixed their minds on the little homestead. A single roan horse, his jowls working a rhythm, mouthing strands of fresh hay, stood in the shade of a corral roof of pine branches adjacent to a modest adobe and log shed.

Within minutes, the sweat-soaked outlaws halted. There was a dark haired woman clad in a buckskin shirt pulled together with rawhide ties, and a deep blue, ankle-length skirt that had come into view beyond the back corner of the cabin. She was scrubbing clothes from a pile that rested on a stack of split firewood half distance between the cabin and stream.

They watched wide-eyed when she drew an arm of clothes from a large wood tub and placed them in another tub atop a wood frame; she began rinsing away soap suds. And then just as quickly, she carried the clothes to a gathering of flimsy, tilted together poles where she spread her handy-work.

The young and well proportioned woman lifted the corner of her skirt and wiped her hands. She stepped back from the fresh laid laundry and pulled an arm across her forehead. Long black hair was tucked recklessly into a drooping pile atop her head and held in place by a matching pair of vivid green combs.

Slats and Jimmy dismounted and lead their horses as they walked toward the corner of the cabin. "She sure 'nuff looks Indian," Jimmy lamented.

"Yep, same woman…she's Shoshone…but part white."

A sly grin parched Jimmy's face, "She's pretty too." His gaze fixed on her bosom, which threatened escape from the tight buckskin.

With her forearm still over her brow, she turned a quarter turn and spoke as if their presence had been expected for some time, "You…are welcome." Her words came slow but firm and deliberate.

Don Russell

"Thank you." Jimmy gestured awkwardly with an open palm, his apprehensive attempt at sign language.

Slats looked about the homey setting, noting a few pinion pines some yards to the rear of the cabin. His eyes stopped at the lean-to at the edge of the corral. A saddle sat on a short chunk of log elevated by legs fashioned from short wood poles. The cautious, adept outlaw saw no signs of the man or boy. However, he took notice of a knife handle extending from the Indian woman's high moccasin, and a lever-action Henry leaning against the cabin near the door.

"We shore could use some grub." Once again Jimmy used hand signs. He held his hand to his chest, "I'm Jimmy," and then swung the hand wide, "this is Slats." The tone and actions were drawn out, presented as if the dark skinned woman couldn't be expected to comprehend.

"Jeemmee." She gave a slight chuckle and then looked at the tall, skinny man, "Slat," she nodded contemptuously to each of them. "You stay…I bring food." With that she started inside. She gave no outward indication of remembering Slats from the lanky outlaw's prior visit to their valley.

"Wait!" Jimmy blurted; he jerked the dirty wide-brim hat from his head and crunched it to his chest. With a childlike awkwardness, he spurted, "What's your name?"

She spun back to face him, her hair unfolded and draped down past her shoulders. The sun exacted the light brass

JIMMY DOSS · OUTLAW

tone of her skin as she turned; it was noticeably pleasing to the rugged blond man. Her facial features were remarkably smooth and delicate.

She stood erect; her posture momentarily exposed an air of defiance, but her lips softened as she said, "My name, Nato-mata-chee...*Eye of Cougar,* in white man tongue." She pulled the door open, "I get food." She disappeared inside, snatching up the rifle as she did so.

"Wonder why she was amused at my name?" Jimmy Doss turned to Slats with a befuddled sneer.

Slats had no idea, but saw the opportunity to belittle his youthful friend; he said, "Well, *Jeemmee,*" he mocked the Indian woman, "sounds like *chimmee,* which in Shoshone, means *little one*! I reckon she's got you pegged, boy," the rope-thin man chided, holding back from showing any indication of humor.

Jimmy's mouth went sour; he said nothing, just stared at the half-open door. Both men stood silently, each absorbing their prospective take on the situation. Jimmy's masculine awareness heightened at the allure of the woman. The gangly man was bent on other possibilities. Slats thought about the new Henry repeating rifle the woman took inside; he knew a gun like that cost plenty, and the saddle over by the lean-to was new also. His mind continued to work as he spoke slow and quietly, "Don't know why a man would buy a wash

tub for his woman when a stream like that is so close…
she probable bathes in that tub too." He was engrossed in
the extravagant manner the prospector bestowed on his
Shoshone squaw-wife.

Jimmy's eyes dropped. They quickly widened as he
visualized what Slats had said about the wash tub. He was
busy with his own thoughts, which were of illusions that
Slats' remark conjured up. He grew fidgety.

"She weren't scared none, was she?" Jimmy's mind was
ripe with fascination of the young woman. The fact she was
Indian confounded his elation. "You reckon she didn't see
us until we walked up on her…maybe," his voice trailed off,
"she was wantin' us to come closer."

"Nope. I'd say she seen us way before we came in sight
of the cabin. She wasn't surprised by us at all – no more
than a mountain lion is surprised when a man walks under
a boulder where he's layin.'"

Both men peered through the partially open door. They
could see Nato-mata-chee's silhouette as she hurried about
inside. The well configured young woman took a steaming
pan from the stovetop and placed it on the ripsaw-crafted
table. She stepped from view momentarily, and then swiftly
returned to the table, where she hastily sliced bread.

The tall, willowy man thought back about the remarks
he'd made when he and his young partner sat atop the

mountain; '*if the man found gold, they'd likely still be there…*
if not, they'd be gone.'

Slats took another look around…no sign of the man or boy. "Let's go inside."

Jimmy didn't hesitate.

CHAPTER SEVEN – JIMMY DOSS, OUTLAW

After crossing the Gila River the lawmen rode northwest in wide patterns, searching for tracks. After an hour they came across the prints, and soon afterward, *horse apples.* The apples were dry. Matt dropped down and broke one open, it was firm but moist inside, "About a day old, I'd say." He looked to the trail ahead, "just the break we needed," he said, tossing it aside, "they're still a day's ride ahead of us."

Matt looked west, to the sun, "We've got two hours of daylight."

"We can't catch them today, and there's not much moon – not enough to track by." The ex-Ranger could tell the two men they followed were confident, or they wouldn't have allowed the sign, and their pace was steady. Hank knew men that killed recently were always dangerous, not to be taken lightly…they would be quick to kill again to escape the law and a neck-stretching.

"You think they feel they played the river good enough that nobody could track them?" Scoot questioned Hank.

"That…and now they're not making effort to cover their trail. I'd say they're more bent on getting to where they're set on, and getting a mite careless in the hurry-up."

Matt gauged Hank's face, "Finding these fellas might be easier than we thought…seems they don't care hob about us or anybody following them."

"I'm not ready to hitch my mule to that plow just yet; sometimes the roughest ground to turn is deeper down." Hank kept his eyes on the mountain pass ahead of them, there'll be a lot of shadows up there in them boulders and pines," he pointed to the pass, "we'll settle on this side for the night and work through there in the morning with the sun at our backs."

The following morning no time was wasted analyzing or questioning horseshoe prints. The pattern was set in Hank's mind. The stage route from Safford to Globe was about fifty miles around the mountain and through the pass beyond. The threesome pushed the horses into a canter. Hank figured if the killers tired or got too careless they might catch them this side of Globe.

Matt could see his friend's jaws flex. He knew the man was set on killing them that shot Josh. The law was leveraged into the man's mind but it wasn't going to stand in his way when the time came; Matt could see it clearly. He remembered Hank telling him that gunfighters nurtured an inner gratification when they killed; he'd heard them say so. Hank also told him that he'd never felt satisfaction when he killed a man, but there wasn't any burdensome feeling either – he'd only killed when he had too, only in keepin' to the law. This time looked to be different. Matt saw the eagerness in his friend and it grieved him, but he'd decided if that's the way it had to be…well, just maybe the hand of the law would settle the matter some how.

Hank Darcy was having some thoughts too. He figured Matt lacked the bank of time where frontier lawmen learned that the execution of justice sometimes was in abrupt resolution. An arrest and courtroom conviction wasn't always the solution – not the best remedy to exact proper punishment. A lawman in this country had to be willing, when the state of affairs prescribed it, for the lawman to serve as judge, jury, and executioner. The Texas Rangers imparted such justice on rare occasions…Matt would have to comprehend and accept that.

Hank thought about Scoot…*'Wish he'd stayed home…he didn't have the sand.'* Hank hardly knew the man before, but he'd been with him for several days now…*'he was too green for this kind of law work'.* Before the actual confrontation with the two killers, Ranger Hank Darcy would find a way force Scoot Wilkins to depart company…if nothing else, if push came to shove, Hank figured to crack a gun barrel over the youngster's head and put him out of the fracas. He'd never need to know what happened, and a man couldn't testify to anything he couldn't possibly witness.

The men rode in silence. Hank kept an eye to the trail and the tracks…this was no time to get careless. *'Overtaking the fugitives somewhere between here and Globe would serve well – away from crowds of people, away from eyewitnesses that couldn't understand'.*

A frontier lawman, provided he lived long enough, developed an extra sense, a sense of comprehension of the man he trailed. They all had traits. Most were just plain mean but others were cunning and stacked with ingenuity – hard to predict. About the time you had a handle on what he would do next, he's alter the pattern and go off on something else.

The sun had slipped past its zenith; it glared down from a vast sky void of clouds. The next three hours would be harsh; or as Hank remembered Josh saying, "The sun's hot enough to melt anything that didn't have the cover of shade." A tinge of satisfaction came to Hank, knowing they buried his younger brother in the shade of the lone sycamore where a breeze always seemed to stir, indifferent from the hot sun.

- -

Slats and Jimmy stormed through the door like a pair of starving coyotes trying to snatch a crippled cottontail.

Nato-mata-chee heard them, having anticipated such. An Indian-raised girl didn't need to see a rattler to know she was about to have the poisonous fangs thrust into her flesh.

She wretched upward and leaped with the dexterity of her namesake, toward the rifle she'd leaned against the table. Weak, macabre sounds surged from her lips, giving notice that she instinctively knew her effort was futile. Her fingers grasped the gun barrel well above the forearm, but it was too late. Slats' strong hand wrapped around her wrist. With a vicious twist he yanked her toward him, her hair flailing and nimble body solely in his control. His other hand, drawn into a rock-hard fist, swished into the side of her face brutally, the impact stung the air like the sound of a beaver tail on hushed pond water.

She went down hard. Her knee struck the plank floor with the kick of a mule and she bounced onto her shoulder before crashing on the side of her head and rolling onto her back, loosing consciousness.

The rifle clattered to the floor and Slats kicked it over to the stone fireplace, well away from the stunned woman.

"Get on her and hold her!" Slats glared furiously at Jimmy as he flung a finger toward the Shoshone girl that was sprawled on the dark floor, her skirt bunched from her knees to her waist.

Before Nato-mata-chee could lift her dazed head, Jimmy was spread-eagle over her on his knees, sitting on her lower stomach. He leaned forward, intending to restrain her hands by clasping her wrists, but hesitated, she was motionless. He let his hands fall to his thighs. Her buckskin shirt was tight against her firm young breasts, her nipples pushing noticeable small swells that drew Jimmy's full attention. Her bosom rose with each breath and the smooth, tawny recess between the gentle mounds showed tiny beads of sweat through the rawhide laces.

Jimmy's eyes moved methodically over her upper body. He realized he'd never before taken notice of the soft flesh of a woman's delicate neck cascading upward to her chin. Nato-mata-chee's lips parted and quivered slightly. A scarlet welt raised on her cheek from the blow struck by Slats. Her head rolled slightly side to side and she moaned softly, involuntarily.

The pretty Indian girl's movements paused, eyelids twitched and then sluggishly opened. Jade green pools, although somewhat glazed, bore into the young man's face. His solemn boyish gaze was filled with sensuality as he straddled Nato-mata-chee and studied her like she was a treasure map. The pleasing oval of her eyes, the arched brows and wisps of fine black hair flowing easily from her temples gave the near-adolescent man unaccustomed warmth, a warmth that was strange to him, but he somehow felt a soothing comfort with it.

The Shoshone girl knowingly looked him square in the face…she wet her lips with a resolutely slow, resourceful sweep of her tongue, measuring Jimmy's intentions and reading the lust he showed like the glow of a full moon on a clear night.

Nato-mata-chee relaxed her body and she smiled meekly, dragging the eager and disheveled figure of young manhood sitting astride her into near total confusion.

Meanwhile the willowy outlaw, on the other side of the room yanked up everything he could lay a hand on, and threw it to the floor. He stopped and glanced back over a shoulder at Jimmy, "She awake?" Slats voice was anxious and sadistic.

Jimmy jerked like he'd been hit with a club. His attention was so focused on the woman under him that he was almost unaware that Slats was wrecking the cabin like a demonic mad man. He looked up, "Yea, yea…she's awake."

"They's got gold here somewhere." Slats jerked bags of flour and coffee from a shelf and slammed them to the floor. He hurriedly examined the contents when he did. He found nothing.

"Get her up…she's gonna show us where the gold is hid."

When Jimmy's attention was averted, Nato-mata-chee's hand slipped to the foot she had drawn up to her hip. She was conscious of the Jimmy's lack of diligence in holding her. She lifted the knife from the top of the tall moccasin and pulled it up to her side. She squeezed the bone handle tightly, arched her back and heaved upward. It threw Jimmy off balance and she plunged the knife toward the right side of his chest.

"Aahhh," Jimmy gasped and flinched. He glimpsed the knife from the corner of his eye and threw his arm skyward to block it.

The blade slashed into his shoulder. "Damn!" His lurch, coupled with the girl's exertion, flung him off her. He thrashed about, cursing and bleeding; his head struck a table leg and an animal-like fury overtook him.

The woman sprang to her feet, gasping and puffing loudly, she stumbled frantically, her head still reeling from the blow Slats had stung her with. Filled with enough anger to cancel the fear, she achieved the bright opening of the door and leaped onto the sun-bleached porch.

"She stabbed me! That bitch stabbed me!" The young outlaw jumped to his feet. He brushed hair from his eyes as he crooked his neck and lifted his arm to see the knife wound inflicted by the enraged Shoshone woman.

'Clang…clang…clang.' Nato-mata-chee wildly wretched the braided rope and the steel bell at the edge of the porch sounded in frantic repetition. The startling sounds beseeched the towering rock formations around the valley with anxious exclamations, announcing a cry for help!

At the third ring, Slats reached her. He grabbed a hand full of black hair with one fist and with the other he crashed the barrel of his revolver across her temple. She went limp without a sound. He released her and she melted into a motionless heap. Blood streamed from the gash and began soaking her ebony hair – she lay silent. The crimson outpouring pumped rapidly, spilled into her ear and down the side of her bronze face. Her life hung by a thread. She'd been battered unwittingly, but her beauty remained apparent.

CHAPTER EIGHT - JIMMY DOSS, OUTLAW

Jimmy staggered to the door. He coughed and growled from irritation and pain as he leaned against the rough wood frame, an arm drawn across his chest, his hand covering the stab wound. He looked at the young Indian woman, fighting the realization that she'd attempted to kill him. He was perplexed, something from inside of him wanting to help her but also angry as hell for what she'd done.

"Damn it, boy!" Slats hand was full of revolver, "I told you to hold her." His breath burst into the boy's face, his voice hot, and long face red with anger. He raised the gun and stuck the end of the barrel within an inch of Jimmy's nose. "If you can't sit on a woman," he hesitated and drew a long breath, "and keep her from cuttin' you, I don't know that you'd be any good to me come a time I'm countin' on you to cover my back." Slats' face contorted, nostrils flared and his eyes bored down on Jimmy's like a branding iron.

"Sorry, Slats." The young man's head dropped. He looked up through locks of greasy blond hair to accept the lanky man's wrath; he swallowed long and hard, his eyes moved from Slats' face to the muzzle of the gun. "It won't ever happen again."

"For damn sure it ain't gonna happen again, and you still be suckin'air." Slats lowered the gun and kept his eyes fixed on Jimmy's. Seconds later his snarled lips steadied and he pushed the gun snug into the holster with the heel of his hand, "Now let's find that gold." He stepped to the edge of the porch and looked up and down the valley as he said, "before that mountain man and his young'n git here. They'll sure 'nuff be coming before long…answerin' that damn bell."

The two men stood in the middle of the cabin's floor. Slats turned away from Jimmy and stared apathetically at the mess he'd made. He turned back momentarily, studied the wound to his young partner's shoulder and reluctantly said, "Let's get that cut bandaged 'for you bleed to death." He reached over to the kerchief hanging loosely around Jimmy's neck, untied it, shook away the dust and dipped it into a bucket of water sitting on the sideboard, wrung it and knotted it into a snug compress. "That'll have to do for now. Maybe the hurtin' will be a lesson."

The angular man went back to the door and looked out at the motionless woman, her blue skirt twisted high up between her legs. A large pool of blood framed her head and shoulders, her eyes were fixed half open, the bright green faded and empty. "Guess I notched her good that time." A crooked smirk came to his face.

"That mountain man and the boy are gonna be coming outta them hills right soon." Slats moved back inside and stood with his hands on his hips, surveying the cabin's contents, his mind set with reasoning where the gold would be. "We'd best find that stash and git over the ridge before that ol' hoot can git us in the sights of that long rifle of his… Cousin Pete said the man could lung-shoot a deer at 'bout six hundred yards."

Jimmy sneered, "Can't nobody do that." He looked at the spindly outlaw with his head cocked, "You afraid of him?" Jimmy chided his friend as he edged toward the door to take another look at the Indian woman. A surly grin came to his lips when he saw her lying motionless, "Maybe we don't need to hurry at all…" He didn't know she was dying.

Slats shook his head in disgust, "Look, boy, you caused this damn mess so don't be givin' me no chin music…there's a time that bein' smart enough to git while the gittin' is good is better than trading lead with a man…sides that, it's one thing to kill a man's woman and another to have to kill his kid."

"Kill a kid...? I don't want no part of that, gold or no gold."

"If you would've held that girl we coulda' had the gold and been outta here. It's your fault; now shut up and look."

Jimmy absorbed the slap of the remark, but felt the wringing-out shouldn't be all on him. "You really think there's gold in here? Shoot, it could be anyplace in them rocks out there – likely not in the house at all," Jimmy snapped his head toward the door.

The long-armed outlaw left nothing untouched, working his way through the log house like a Texas tornado, throwing everything he handled. Ten minutes of searching, racked with breaking up everything he got his hands on, jerking and staggering, he finally stood quiet in the middle of it all. He knew rummaging longer was useless – maybe the gold was somewhere outside like Jimmy said. He grabbed the boy outlaw by the collar and yanked him out the door – he was madder than hob – he wouldn't forget.

- -

"Up there?" Scoot Wilkins stared open-mouthed at the mountainside, knowing Hank had his sights set to climb.

"They did…so we are too." Hank's voice was matter-of-fact. "Their trail is plain as following a bull through fresh plowed ground. They sure don't care if they leave sign…all along they seem to be sure of direction." He continued to stare up the rock-strewn slope…"Don't know what this is about, but they're pretty much certain 'bout their route."

"Could be a set-up for a bush-whackin'," Scoot threw in, "don't make sense otherwise."

"That ain't it, they feel sure no one's on their tail – they could have set us up more than a couple of dozen times before now if they'd wanted." Hank continued his glare up the mountainside, "A man never knows what he'll find until he rides to the other side."

"Whatever you say, Hank, Scoot and I are following your lead." Matt knew the ex-Ranger was right and the respect he had for the man's knowledge of tracking outlaws wasn't questionable. Matt raised his hand to read the sun, "We've got several hours of daylight. If them two made it up that slope, we can."

They leaped and gouged their way up the mountainside, half the time tugging on reins to keep the horses moving higher up when the footing was too soft. Scrabble of sandy soil and stones rolled down behind them; large rocks skipped and bounced clean to the cluster of white-bark aspens hundreds of feet below. When they reached the top they were worn and weary from the hot sun. Surprised but pleased, they saw the spacious valley and winding stream a few hundred feet below. Matt said what each of them was thinking, "Well, will you look at that!"

"I'd say those boys knew what was here," Hank rolled his hat brim and flagged the dust from his clothes, "This is either where they was headed…or maybe a short cut they knew. We best keep our eye peeled, could be we're close." He flipped a thumb back where they'd made the climb, "I've been up and down enough mountains and seen enough slides, that one wasn't no act of nature. Someone put powder to that hill, more than a little, I'd say. Seems someone don't want nobody coming up the climb for some reason or another."

"Why in God's name would they do that – way out here?" Scoot stepped up on a colorless boulder the size of a wagon and made measure of the valley.

He took in the pines that rimmed the valley up high and then fell scattered to the stone-lined stream cascading through tall grass that bent spasmodically with breezes in the quiet below. He threw an arm shoulder high and pointed, "Look, there's a stem of smoke risin' up behind the rock outcropping - over there where the wide arc in the stream bides yonder!"

The other two men snapped their heads to Scoot's outcry and followed the direction his finger jabbed the air. All stood in silence for a few seconds.

"You think we caught 'em?" Matt searched Hank's face for the answer.

At first, everyone had the same thought. But Hank considered the man-made mountain slide, "Could be…or maybe we'll find out who don't want nobody using this trail." Hank studied the thin wisp of smoke, watching as it slowly scattered with the breeze, "That ain't no camp fire… more like chimney," he turned and grabbed the reins. He stepped a toe into the stirrup, "Let's go see. You two…spread a few yards behind me, and keep your eyes open."

The three men started off with tense anticipation. They descended the steep grade guardedly in single-file and near the tree line. The valley floor was within a few hundred feet. The tall rock formation hiding the origination of the tendril of smoke was maybe four hundred yards to the right of a small rise that bent the creek.

Hank violently jerked from the saddle, his black hat spun into the air and the big black reared, fighting the jolt of hard yanked reins. The boom of a long gun, followed by echoes reverberating through the valley left no question… Hank Darcy had been shot! He thumped to the hard ground like a steer shot for slaughter.

Matt Ragle leaped from his horse and held to the reins, taking cover behind a small Mexican white pine. Scoot followed. Squatting low behind the tree with bridle reins in hand, they scanned the valley below. A small fog of powder smoke rose over a knot of rocks three hundred yards away. Matt looped the leather strapping over a limb and turned to Scoot, "You sit tight, I'm going after Hank."

The young sheriff stooped low and quickly worked forward with choppy steps, the few yards to where Hank laid on his side, his arm flung upward, covered the side of his head. Matt first saw the blood on the sandy soil...and then on the shirt, "Oh, God, no!"

He pushed the shirt collar aside to get a better look. Hank groaned hoarsely and his hand moved slightly, as if the were trying to fight...but a single heave of air flushed from him and he went as limp as a coil of old rope. "Hank!" Matt called out in a guarded tirade. No response.

Hank's horse had moved to the downhill side of the fallen ex-Ranger, stamped and nickered. "Good boy." Matt grasped a rein, speaking to quiet him. He turned Hank onto his back and took both of the Ranger's hands in his. He dug in his heels and scooted on his backside, dragging the man to the cover of rocks and squatty pines a few feet uphill, all the while expecting another boom to clamor through the valley. But there was none.

CHAPTER NINE – JIMMY DOSS, OUTLAW

Matt settled both himself and Hank into a depression out of the shooter's sight. He lifted the dark wavy hair from the side of Hank's head. It was a slicing wound; blood flowed freely with each heart beat. But he was alive. If the bullet had struck a half inch to the left his skull would likely have been shattered.

A deep, blustery voice yelled from down in the valley, "You up there – you'd best load up your kilt friend and git the hell 'way from here. If'n you don't, I'll kill the lot of ya."

The angry voice of a child shrieked, "We kill all of you – you tried to kill my ma!"

"What in tarnation…?" Matt turned to Scoot, who had crept forward to where Matt had dragged Hank, "That's a kid!" They looked at each other, bewilderment and confusion etched in their faces. Matt's mind leaped back to the time he was a teenager caught stealing rifles in Dumas. Shame filled him; he'd wished he was someone else, anywhere else - it all seemed unreal. That same feeling engulfed him now. He shook his head to clear the cobwebs.

"Hank's lost a lot of blood…we gotta do something." Matt held his fingers against the side of the wounded man's neck, "Pulse is weak. We can't just sit here and let him die."

Scoot peeked over the rocks cautiously. 'I'm going to work my way over there," he pointed, "maybe I can see who did the yellin', and how many there are down there."

"You'd best be real careful, whoever it is, is good with that long gun."

"Hold on here, Matt, I'll be back." Scoot took his hat in his hand and slowly bellied out of the concaved area.

Matt wormed his way a few feet to where his horse was tied and retrieved a canteen from his haversack. He slid back to where Hank laid, pulled the cork and poured water into the wound. There was a slice in the flesh over Hank's ear the size of man's thumb. He ripped away a piece of Hank's blood soaked shirt collar, drenched it and compressed the damp cloth into the wound. He then rolled his neck kerchief lengthwise and tied it around Hank's head Indian fashion.

There was no telling how long he might be unconscious. Matt had once seen a man with a bad head wound lie in oblivion for more than a week, and when he did wake up he didn't even remember his own name. Too much movement or a sudden lurch could cause the rupture of blood vessels on the surface of the brain, resulting in permanent brain impairment, or death.

It was a long twenty minutes before Matt saw Scoot awkwardly crab-walking back. The afternoon sun dropped to where the shadows were beginning to grow long. The people down below had made no more threats or sounds of any kind. The only noises were the scrapping sounds made by Scoot and the rasping of crows from distant trees.

"There's a cabin down there; evidently those folks live there." Scoot pulled the cork on the canteen and took a couple of hurried swallows. "The kid said something about us tryin' to kill his ma...my guess is that the two men we trailed here did it, and they think we're tied in with them in some way."

"Makes sense...but what are we gonna do about it? We ain't in much shape to put up an argument." Matt lifted his head for another look down into the valley.

"This side of the cabin, about sixty yards, I saw a man with a face full of whiskers; he's holdin' a rifle with a barrel near four feet long...must be the gun what shot Hank – how is he anyway?"

75

"He ain't good – ain't moved neither; his breathing is unsteady, but I got the bleeding stopped." Matt took a minute to study Hank, and then rose again to look below. "We can't stay here, and we shore can't go back down that rockslide of a mountain. Hank couldn't handle it." The young sheriff had calmed himself but he was completely aware that his best friend's life was in his hands.

Sheriff Ragle hated the circumstance. He was a lawman that confronted an adversary as he had done with the three bank robbers back in town. There he'd taken a stance to shoot it out with them. That was his way; stand up to trouble head on. If you didn't, your enemy could gain strength and confidence. But if he saw you didn't fear him the edge could turn to you.

"So what we gonna do, Matt?"

"Well, I been thinking…about the only thing we can do is, I gotta go down there. The longer we sit here the worse it is for Hank."

"And just how you gonna do that? The man said he'll kill us."

Matt paid no mind to Scoot's comment, and he avoided looking the second time at the twisted intensity in the deputy's face. "I'm gonna slip down close as I can – I believe I can move down there, where them little pines are." He pointed to a spot a hundred yards or so ahead and a little left where a small wad of boulders the size of barrels sat in the shade of a dozen young pine trees.

Scoot studied Matt for an instant; he knew from the look on his face that he was going to do what he'd just said. Trying to talk him out of it would only create a row between them. That would add to their predicament. Reluctance was in the deputy's voice when he said, "You might make it if you crawl." Scoot had some doubt but knew it was no use to say otherwise, so he added, "You'd best not stick your head up, that old man can sure enough shoot that cannon...you saw what he can do...I got no hankerin' to go back to Silver City and become sheriff."

"Thanks...I appreciate your encouragement." Matt gave a giddy grin and laid his hat aside as he dropped to his belly, "I'm taking my rifle. If they don't stand to reason..." he hesitated, "I reckon I'll be close enough to make a fight of it. That kid being in the fray complicates things; seems the whole deck is stacked against us."

He held the rifle crossways in his elbows and started crawling. He worked around the manzanitas and bearberry, and stayed behind the cover of sage and rocks as best he could.

Several long minutes later he reached the protection of the shaded rock formation, evidently never being seen – no shots were fired. He sat up slowly and raised his head. He could see the cabin, but not the man with the long gun or the kid. Matt dusted debris from his arms and checked the Winchester to be sure there was no dirt to hinder the action. He raised his head a bit more, "Hello down there!"

No response called back. But he knew they'd heard him – if they were still there…and he knew they could tell he had advanced toward them. He gave the thought a minute for them to get used to and then spoke again, louder this time, "We're the law up here…from over Silver City." He waited for an answer.

There was none.

Matt cupped his hands at his cheeks, directing his voice, "We been following two outlaws…we know they came this way…probably not more than a few hours ago."

For what seemed an eternity, all was quiet. And then, the growl from the man down-slope called back, "You say yer the law?"

"That's right, the law from Silver City…we're after two outlaws that robbed the bank and killed four men."

Matt listened. After several seconds without a reply, he cupped his hands and shouted again, "We're trailing two outlaws…we know they came this way, their tracks are fresh and looks like they headed for your cabin." Matt waited. "You shot my friend…he's hit bad."

"Is he dead?" The growl had lost its' viciousness.

"Your bullet gouged the side of his head, but he's alive."

Another minute passed. "How do I know yer the law?"

The talk between the two was slow and deliberate, each man thinking cautiously, weighing what was said. Two or three more minutes of quiet passed.

"I saw three of you'ens up there…all ya the law?"

"That's right. All of us are lawmen."

It was quiet again.

An idea came to Matt. Back in Amarillo he and Hank had been confronted by a man whose father had been shot down by masked night-riders. The man was understandably doubtful when the lawmen rode into the yard following the murder – he was mad and dangerous – and well armed. Hank figured the man would respect the law once he was convinced they intended no harm, only to help. Hank told the man what he was going to do, and then dropped his guns in view of the desperate man and backed toward him, his hands held high in the air and his law badge vividly displayed in one of them. It worked.

Matt's allegiance to Hank was enormous, he had to do something. He'd have to trust his competence to convince the man with the long gun that he was being up-front with him. And in turn Matt would have to trust the whiskered man not to shoot! Matt figured both his life and Hank's was at stake – perhaps Scoot's as well.

And if it didn't work, who would know; this is wild country. People die out here, hundreds of them that are never reported or even known. Unmarked graves lie beneath the earth's crust all over the West, not to mention the people who never got buried, those whose bones dried up and decayed after being stripped clean by coyotes and vultures.

Matt took a deep breath. He yelled, "I'm going to show you…we are the law. I'm going to stand up; you'll see my badge…and I'll not be armed." He took another very deep breath, stood, hands lifted high with his badge catching the full light of the sun. Very slowly he laid the rifle on the rock at his side and then, still very slowly, he lifted the pistol from the holster and laid it next to the rifle. "Look, I'm leaving my guns…got no gun…my badge is in my hand." He deliberately waved the hand holding the sheriff star. "I'll back up so's you know I'm no threat, and I'm telling the God's truth."

The whiskered man stepped out from behind the boulder, "Walk slow, boy. This here Sharps will be pointed square between yer shoulders; couldn't miss ya if I tried… and I shore wouldn't try."

"Go 'head and shoot 'em, Pa!" The boy had walked to his father's side and watched. His teeth were clinched behind snarled lips as Matt Ragle began inching his way backward down the hillside.

"No, son. We don't kill no man what we don't know needs killin'. This here man is either crazy'ern a bedbug or tellin' the truth. I'm believin' he's tellin' us the truth." A short minute passed. Isaiah took his eye from Matt long enough to look into the eyes of his son, "Yer ma was hurt a spell afore you saw these here men up the hill and come to tell me about 'em comin. I don't believe they would've been coming this way slow like they was if they'd done the harm to your ma." Isaiah looked at the boy with fatherly compassion, "I'm thinking I shouldn'ta shot when I did. She did tell us it was two fellers, not three."

The broad-shouldered mountain man set the butt of the long gun on the ground, holding it upright beside him. He watched Matt continue to work down the slope awkwardly, hands still above his head and one of them holding the shinning badge.

The dark-haired youngster squinted down his eyes, anger still very much alive within him. But he also accepted the reasoning his pa gave. The Shoshone within him respected the truth and strength Matt showed. It did little, however, to fill the need he wrestled with in his gut; the need to avenge the near death condition of his ma.

CHAPTER TEN –
JIMMY DOSS, OUTLAW

The next morning, as the top of the sun edged over the peaks, Matt and Scoot stood next to Hank's makeshift bed in the rear of the cabin. They sipped coffee. Few words were spoken between them. Hank Darcy breathed deeply but finally lay quiet; a cloth bandage covered a portion of his head. He'd spent a restless night, heavy with thrashing and grumbles.

The lean-to addition of the mountain family's home sheltered the lifeless body of Nato-mata-chee, lying atop a well-groomed deer hide. The blow Slats struck with his pistol broke through her skull. It was decisive. Isaiah dressed her for burial in a soft, near-white buckskin dress. He'd braided her hair and decorated the braids with porcupine quills and beads. She had occasionally outfitted herself with the beads and quills as she sat with her son, John Eagle-Heart, telling him of her family and the homeland where she's been raised. Even in death, the Shoshone girl's beauty was clearly perceptible.

Nato-mata-chee had awakened briefly before midnight. And in barely audible words passing through her lips, she etched the names, "Slats" and "Chimmee". Isaiah didn't fully understand the words his dying wife spoke, but Matt Ragle told him of the men he, Hank, and Scoot were trailing.

She'd also said, "No find gold."

Isaiah Worsham had hidden two small pokes of gold dust and another bag half filled with small nuggets in a pair of metal boxes tucked up under a steel brace on the bottom of the stove. Nato-mata-chee had built a fire in the stove when she first saw Slats and Jimmy top the rise above the valley. She knew a fire would dissuade a man from placing his hand against a hot stove searching, if they were to become so inclined. She'd given her life for her husband and son. They could live the life Isaiah had always related in the 'Land of Plenty', as she understood the many descriptions he'd told to her and her son, 'John-motah-toska', in Shoshone.

Last night the only light in the cabin was the shallow essence of yellow from two candles, one near Nato-mata-chee, and the other one next to Hank Darcy. Now, in the daylight of the morning sun, sadness filled the room as completely as the previous night's darkness.

John Eagle-Heart went to Hank's bedside and seemed to study the man intently, perhaps believing his death was eminent; he then went out the door and stood silently looking into the distance, beyond the pines and the mountain tops.

Matt joined Isaiah and the boy on the front porch. Stillness was broken when Isaiah asked the lawman about the men he pursued. Matt filled in details of the robbery and the killing of the three men, giving descriptions from the information Marsh Halstead had related to him and Hank before they left Silver City. The whiskered man asked about the "very tall" outlaw and related that a similar man had visited the mountain family a couple or three years in the past – he wondered if perhaps it'd been the same man. The boy lifted his big green eyes, first to Matt and then to his father, his expression questioning the words of the two men as they ambled toward the porch out front.

The hefty-framed mountain man took a seat in the rocking chair and put a match to his pipe, his son stood at his side. The lines at the corner of the man's eyes deepened and became rimmed with redness; he sniffed from time to time. John held a hand on his father's forearm and mostly looked at his own feet. When he did look at Matt, his stare bore through, and then suddenly jerk away when his green eyes began to glisten.

The afternoon sky darkened with an eerie silence. A slight breeze brushed the tall grass at the valley's floor on either side of the stone-lined stream. The crows that appeared in the lofty pines yesterday reappeared, but in greater number; and as quiet today as they were noisy the previous day.

With Matt's help, Isaiah and John buried Nato-mata-chee a few paces east of the cabin. They placed the bell she'd rung as her last act in life, on a flat gray stone at the head of her grave. Isaiah said it would ring out to the Great Spirit to come and fetch up her spirit, saving her soul from the evils of the white man; John nodded in agreement.

It had been three days since the mountain man's slug from the long gun crashed into the side of Hank's head. Hank was resting easy now, though still unconscious, the previous two days he had a fever and jerked about wildly, having to be restrained. During the third day the fever diminished and bits of spasmodic twitching replaced the wildness. Herbal packing that Isaiah prepared, a Shoshone medicine taught to him by his woman, seemed to ease swelling from the wound. Hank's eyelids had fluttered but never opened, and a throaty groan was translated as a possibility he was about to regain consciousness.

"What are we gonna do, Matt? We just gonna sit here and wait for him to come around or…?" Scoot Wilkins voice faded but he had already stated the thoughts that had been running through Matt Ragle's mind for the past several hours, since sun-up.

"I ain't for sure. I'm thinking we give him another day – maybe two," Matt scratched at his cheek, "then if he don't come around, we'll make that decision." The sheriff sat on a chair and leaned forward, elbows on his thighs, staring at Hank.

The whiskered mountain man and the eight year old boy sauntered over to the foot of Hank's bed, Isaiah said in a hush, "You fellas want to go on after them killers, I'm all for ya to. Me and John will be gatherin' things together…" He jerked his head toward the mountainside the visitors had ascended to reach the valley, "And I'm gonna put some more charges into that old trail yonder – don't need no more trouble comin' up thata way."

Matt and Scoot looked at one another, remembering what Hank had said about someone blasting the mountain, no natural landslide to lay blame on.

"We goin' after them, Pa?" John questioned his father, having heard him speak of watching after Hank if Matt and Scoot went on.

I'm thinkin' on it, son." He gazed down at the youngster knowing the boy's thoughts…he wanted to kill the men who'd killed his mother. "A man can't let his innards do the thinkin' for him; it'll get him in trouble shore as lightnin' chases down a thunderstorm. Nope, a man best think with

his head, not his heart…he'd best know where the lightnin'
is likely to be afore he charges out inta the rain!"

- -

Slats McClary and Jimmy flushed from the valley within
minutes once Nato-mata-chee rang the warning bell and
they'd hastily made a vain search. They hardly exchanged
words once they'd mounted up, each of them being lost in
their own thoughts. Slats had seen evidence of bounty, the
rifle, the saddle, supplies, even the wash tub, but he was
forced to leave with only a few of the mountain man's cigars
and six sticks of dynamite, not an ounce of gold. He laid the
blame on his young outlaw partner who'd fizzled in efforts
to keep the Indian girl under control.

The vision of that alluring, bronze-skinned woman, her
soft body, deep green eyes and supple line of her lips, stuck
in Jimmy's mind like barbwire grows into a tree it had been
nailed to. He scarcely realized the saddle was under him.
The buckskin gelding followed Slat's horse without so much
as prodding of the knees or touch of leather on his neck.
Slats occasionally looked back at Jimmy's empty stare, shook
his head and swore under his breath. Globe and Cousin Pete
weren't far up ahead, and the money in the saddlebags held
more future possibilities than the empty-headed kid. But
Slats had come to have a liking for the boy, even though he
was void of coming up with a reason for feeling that way.

The two men pulled up at the bank of a creek. Slats slid down, knowing he needed to get Jimmy's mind brought up to where they were, some distance away from the valley and the girl, "Horses gotta have a blow and need water. I figure Globe to be about four miles up the trail." Slats tossed a half bottle of whiskey to Jimmy, "Take a couple of pulls on this, partner…you gotta clear your head. What's done is done and can't be took back." Slats could see Jimmy's mind was still filled with clumsy thoughts of the green-eyed girl, "Look here, boy, we got money – lots of it…We'll get us one of them smell-good-ladies with frillies all over, one with pretty blond curly hair full of ribbons! What ya say?" Slats grinned.

Jimmy nodded his head, more to please Slats than to agree with him. He pushed the bottle to his lips, taking in the whiskey, the hot glow moved down his chest swallow after swallow. The warmth of Nato-mata-chee beneath him and the soft flow of her body began to dissipate in the fog of his mind, but he'd remember, he told himself…for the rest of his life he'd remember.

The skinny, long-legged outlaw made an attempt to rearrange his partner's thinking, "I believe we're close enough to Globe that I can almost smell chimney smoke." He maneuvered the gray next to Jimmy's horse, close enough that their stirrups clanked, "Had me a gal in Globe last time…Whooee, she was a beauty…and did she know how to please a man." Slats clicked his cheek and winked at Jimmy. "If she's still there, I guarantee you, boy, you'll forget everything – even your name – once she pulls them covers over her head."

Jimmy looked up wryly at Slats' big smiling face, and then glanced beyond him. He saw a church bell-tower in the distance that jutted above the trees. As if coming out a trance, he yelled, "Let's go find your curly headed blond gal!" He flung the bottle against a rock, slapped spurs into his mount and rocked forward in the saddle, aiming toward Globe like a man half possessed by the devil.

"Hold up there, Jimmy." Slats grabbed at the bridle of Jimmy's horse and nearly yanked the bit clear of the animal's mouth.

The boyish outlaw gave Slats a hard look, his eyes simmering with fire, "You'd best let go, Slats...I've had about all the pappyin' I'm gonna take from you."

The slender man's hand went to his six-shooter and was in Jimmy's face before he hardly knew what had happened. "Look here, boy, I ain't taken you to raise...if you keep actin' like a apron-grabbin' school kid, I'd as soon be rid of you as not." Slats thumbed the hammer back on the Russian .44 and snarled at the kid, "You best listen to me and listen good." Their horses came together with a jolt, but Slats gun stayed close to the young blond man's nose, "I'm tryin' hard to put some brains in that noggin of yours – but if you keep on this way I'd just as soon put a bullet in there instead." Slats' teeth clinched as he flashed the gun square in the boy's face, "Boy, you got some makins' of a fair partner but you gotta settle a bit…ain't no man gonna ride with me and act like a damn fool."

Jimmy's face caved in and his shoulders slumped – he was sorry he smarted off. What Slats was saying had some stock in it; Jimmy had let the Indian woman pack his head full of honeybees and they'd been hummin' around in there for quite a spell, "You're right, Slats." His eyes fell slowly from the gun in his face to his hands atop the horn. His thoughts traced back a few seconds to where Slats referred to him as 'a partner'. The young man hadn't realized how important it was to him. He let the words flow through his mind again, and again. The warmth he felt, of being a part of something, of being wanted by someone, he liked.

Back in Missouri, near Tipton, where Jimmie had been raised by an aunt and uncle since he was eleven and his folks had died, he had never felt wanted. The uncle worked for the Butterfield Stage Line, being gone sometimes a week or more. He was there to do chores, help with the milking, planting, and the like – but he never felt to be a part of the family.

CHAPTER ELEVEN - JIMMY DOSS, OUTLAW

Globe was abuzz. Dozens of people busied the streets and boardwalks; miners packing tools, no-accounts blowin' smoke, womenfolk of different sorts, some shoppers, gamblers, and rowdies wastin' away the clock. They made the town rival the appearance of a back-east city.

Four men in catalog-type clothes come out of the bank. One had a fist wrapped around a stack of currency. Each of them was glad-handing one another, laughing and no doubt heading for a celebration of sorts as they readily stepped up and entered the *Jubilee Saloon*.

The outlaw twosome sat their saddles lazy-like, silently taking in the activities and mixture of social consortiums. "Some town, huh," Slats words and big grin seemed to awaken the younger man from thought.

"Yea…some town," Jimmy's response was both questionable and gratuitous.

On Slats last visit to Globe the town exposed only a barren, roughshod collection of ripped canvas tents, one small wood frame hotel, a hardware, a blacksmith and a dozen adobe or rock structures, principally saloons. The round globe-shaped silver-laden hunk of ore the town came to be named after hadn't been more than five months out of the ground. Back then most of the population was busy at their claims with picks and shovels, keeping to themselves. When the scatter of men weren't sweating with back-breaking work, or drinking in the saloons, they were in the brush hunting. Food quickly became scarce.

Slats spoke up, "I think the both of us could use a mite of scrubbing….take the itch out of our britches and give the flies a hankerin' for the livery rather than hang onto our saucy smells."

Jimmy Doss dropped his nose toward his chest, sniffed and gave unhurried nods, "I reckon those gals will have to wait just a bit longer." His eyes fixed on a stripped barber pole a few doors down the street. "I believe you're right, Pappy, a little soakin' and some lye soap would make me irresistible." For the first time since leaving the mountain valley and the Indian girl, happiness built an expression in his face.

The lanky man glared at the boy, not knowing how to take his *Pappy* remark.

"Hey, out there," Slats barked as he lifted the dark cigar from his lips, "them clothes ready yet?" He sat in a large wooden tub with soap-stained water to the middle of his chest, "And this water is chillin'…you hear me?"

Jimmy sat in a tub next to him. "You don't reckon that China-boy stole our clothes do you?" His smile professed an attempt at humor. "I'm thinkin' nearly an hour woulda' give them plenty time to wash and press a couple of shirts and pants and the like, don't you?"

The door to the tub room swung open, a petite girl with slanted eyes, hair drawn back snug against her head and bound into a rope-like tail at the back, stepped into the room with fresh laundered clothes. She stood in wood soled shoes that peeked beneath a full, deep red, green and brown brocade skirt. She bowed repeatedly toward the men submerged in lukewarm water. Their mouths hung open. They bowed back to her as she placed the clothes in a stack on a table in the corner before backing out of the door, smiling and bowing.

"Well…I'll be!" Slats had a smirk chiseled into his face, "Looks like the women folks in this town are anxious to see us, boy." Having said that he stepped from the tub and wrapped a towel around his waist.

"I'll not keep 'em waitin'." Jimmy hurriedly separated his clothes and dressed. His blond hair held tones of gold; the encrusted grime was washed away for the first time in days. His face looked younger, the dark shadow of whiskers scraped away by a barber with a straight razor while he sat soaking.

Slats too, took on an invigorating look. He dressed, stooped and craned his neck in front of a mirror, palming his chin and cheeks. He was clean shaven for the first time in more than two weeks, "Well, there's a right handsome man...smells good too." He snatched up the saddlebags he'd draped over the tub and he and young Jimmy made their way through the barber shop and onto the street.

"I'll be taking my share outta them bags now, Slats," said Jimmy.

Slats nodded inappreciably and locked his eyes on the wooden two-story building across the street. It was freshly painted dark green, shutters and doors trimmed with brown. The sign said *'Emerald Hotel and Café'*. He pointed, "Let's go over there."

Still several feet from the counter Jimmy snapped at the desk clerk, "Two rooms."

"Make that one room... with two beds, overlooking the street." Slats punched the back of a fist into Jimmy's stomach and the clerk knew that would be the final word on the matter. Slats figured on keeping an eye on the youngster. He'd give him limited free-reign – but not enough to hang the both of them. He dipped the pen into the inkwell and signed 'Kendrick McClary', followed by the number two, and paid for a week's stay.

"This'll do fine," Slats remarked as he lifted the flimsy curtain at the street-front window. The view was more than a hundred yards up the street, saloons and gambling halls dominated; some that advertised 'dance girls' caught his eye. "Tell ya what, Jimmy, I'm divyin' up half of your cash to ya is all for now…I don't want you to tie on a big drunk and waste it all in the first whorehouse you land in today – the rest of your share I'll hold for safe keepin'. And, boy, you best allow that shoulder of yours to heal before you bite off mor'n you can chew." With that Slats laid the saddlebags on a bed and unbuckled one side.

Jimmy stared at the back of the tall Irishman's head – his first thought was that the skinny man might need a hard thump on his head to loosen the grip he'd taken on the whole money situation. But he quickly worked through the disadvantages that might come from that…and instead, adjusted both his gun belt and his thinking. He also recalled that Slats had spoken of *seed money* being required – to make them rich for the rest of their lives.

"There, that's two thousand dollars," Slats slammed the cash into Jimmy's chest with enough force that the anxious youngster flinched and buckled, "and for God's sake don't let some frilly woman take it away the first day in town." He took a step back and read the candy-store-look on Jimmy's face, "Why don't you put a thousand in your boot," Slats added, "and don't take your boots off."

The young boy from Missouri did – he removed a boot and layered bills along the sole, put the boot back on and dropped cash down inside. "Don't worry about me ole man, I've been to the city before – even went off to Kansas City once." He stomped the boot to the floor to shuffle the bills down, "And I spent a couple days in Wichita before I found you down in El Paso. I know my way around…but ain't never had this kind of money to enjoy with." Jimmy left the door standing open as he hit the hallway. He slid the toes of his boots up and down the back of his pant legs and tugged the hat brim down a mite before he arrived at the stairs.

Slats pulled back the mattress and laid short stacks of bills in neat rows. He loaded his pockets with various denominations of bills and left some of the cash in the saddlebags along with the six sticks of dynamite. He stuffed that in the bottom drawer of the chest of drawers. "Well, I don't suppose I'm gonna see that boy till sometime tomorrow," he said to himself as he took another look out the window. Afterward he unbuckled one of the Russian

.44's and placed it in the middle drawer. "Let's see just how much this town has growed up," he pushed the door shut behind him and locked it.

Cutthroats and card sharks, together with the saloon doves, were not in short supply. The lot of them, along with the whiskey tenders, made their way by separating the men from their day's diggings, usually before midnight, most every day of the week. Nearly every man-jack in Globe had a revolver strapped to his side, in a pocket or boot, or stuffed behind his belt under a coat. The store clerks, carpenters, livery rakers and even mule cart handlers were made up of the men who'd hoped to strike it rich but had to relinquish their dreams and take on whatever job they could find just to eat – or gather together another stake and go back to find their prosperity in the next hole their destiny led them to.

Slats had made a life of hoodwinking and stealing. It didn't take him long to decide this was a place where a shrewd man could pull together a sizeable poke. His cousin, Pete Murray, had been here for three years now, and he was a man that knew how to find the ripest fruit in the orchard. The rail-like outlaw stood on the boardwalk in front of the *Emerald*. He was amazed at the collective changes that had transformed the quiet little mining town into the muddled hodgepodge of wretched greed and disillusion that it had become in a brief span of time.

Slats scratched a match on the post and lit a fresh five cent cigar, *"Well, Pete, where might you be in this hell-hole of a town?"* He started off down the boardwalk, determined to stay on the boards rather than indulge in the grubby traffic that filled the streets.

CHAPTER TWELVE – JIMMY DOSS, OUTLAW

Daylight faded into dusk. The slender Irishman had been in a dozen saloons and turned away multiple ambitions to be entertained by painted ladies in upstairs chambers. He sat for a few hands of stud poker even though he'd judged it best to remain a reserved stranger until he had conversation with Cousin Pete. Pete's letter indicated that his plan would involve a certain amount of chicanery…a common element of his cousin's business practices, as Slats remembered.

Late afternoon brought more activity to the Friday hubbub. Miners, with mud-stained boots and befouled shirts and trousers had become more plentiful when the sun sat on the ridge overlooking the west end of town. Slats lit another nickel cigar and considered whether to return to *The Emerald Hotel,* or make another round of saloons and try to find Jimmy, when his eye caught a sign across the street, *Royal Globe Saloon*; not just the saloon, but a sign jutting out from over a doorway adjacent to the saloon; *Irish Pete's Loan Office.*

Slats crossed the street, staying clear of the mud, on the lengthy, unsteady boards. He leaned his long frame back as he looked up to reread the sign that hung over an open doorway and staircase that lead to another door at the top of the stairs. The tall Irishman grinned, "Yep, this must be his." He put a toe on the first step. As he did so the door at the top of the stairs jerked open and a man came through it, flying head first.

"And don't come back ya Scottish bum unless ya got yourself a paper-filed claim." Pete's head appeared. Locks of red hair flung to one side and a short fat cigar protruded from wide lips under a bushy moustache. It was him alright, nasty temper and all.

Holding his lean frame aside, Slats poked his head through the doorway and watched the man bounce down the stairs with arms and legs flailing.

Cousin Pete's eyes latched onto Slats as the man he'd heaved down the stairs flew through the doorway. "Glory be! Kendrick! That you?"

"Yep, it's me."

"Well, get your behind up here, you long bag of bones!"

Slats shook his head and took to the steps, two at a time. "You ole pirate, I come like ya asked."

"Gosh Almighty, it's good to see ya, cuz." Pete held the door wide, smirking and grinning, his eyes flashed over rosy cheeks, moustache, and bloated nose.

Once the two did their back slapping and exchanged personal insults, Pete yanked a bottle of rye from a desk drawer and the cousins spent time well into the night talking of old times, of family and the like. Slats' and Pete's mothers were sisters, coming to America with their parents as young girls when they were but ten and twelve years old. The girls' mother had died of the fever within six weeks after processing through immigration. The sisters, along with their fathers, remained in New York and both married good Irish men from the upper Bronx, one named McClary and the other named Murray.

"We shore enough had us some times, Kendrick." Pete laughed and yo-yoed his head. Unlike Slats, Pete was on the burly side of big, but like Slats, he loved the dicey, chancy side of life, moved around considerably – not always of his choosing, but regularly anyhow. He'd stayed in Globe longer than he'd been anywhere else since Memphis, and that was back when he was still a young man in his twenties.

The bottle of rye whiskey was wrung out and the cigar ashes grew into heaps before Slats said, "Now, what about this *seed money,* cousin?"

"Did ya bring it?" Pete leaned forward and pushed his rusty moustache up with his lower lip.

"Yep, just like you asked…didn't I always come through when we was kids?"

"You always did and that's why I sent you that letter, Kendrick."

"I wish you'd drop that *Kendrick* stuff and call me by the name your pappy gave me when I was hiding under the bed."

"Yea, you was hiding alright, cause your pa was fixin' to tan yer hide…but he found you easy enough cause your feet was stickin' out – you was too tall even back then…I think you was, what, maybe ten or eleven years old?"

The two men had grown up more like brothers than cousins. Like all things, time changes and people change, but the two of them had always shared a strong bond. That was the ingredient that brought them back together once again, a bond of trust, confidence and dependability on one another.

The conversation, which had been about old times and fun, shifted…the rinky-tink piano music from the *Royal Globe Saloon* had subsided and the clock moved past its' zenith when Pete's face firmed, his eyes locked on the cigar he tapped with a finger as he held it over the deep blue dish brimming with ashes, "We got us some real opportunity here, Kendrick...uuhhh, Slats, and I figure you're the man that can work with me to make it happen."

"Like I said, Cousin Pete, you can count on me."

The bulky Irishman drew a deep breath and started, "I got me a close friend here in Globe, near to like a silent partner, a man by the name of Rink Slater. He owns the *Royal* next door. We got us a secret door between this place and his office." Pete pointed to a large bookcase that dominated the wall behind him. "That swings open and, glory be to the magic of the little people, there's a passageway to the back of a closet in Rink's office. It's been right handy time to time."

Irish Pete Murray threw his large rounded shoulders backward into the tufted leather chair and turned to face the bookcase. "I do a good bit of poker playin' over there and have found a need to leave the game early on occasion... right handy for that," his laugh left little to the imagination. "Well, me and Rink...," Pete threw a thumb in the air indicating the bookcase again, "well, I was planning to put him into this if you didn's show up, but that card don't need to be played now. What I was really needin' was a man who's not known in this town to throw in with me – that'd be you. Rink's my best friend, but he ain't our blood, ya know what I mean."

Slats thumb-nailed a match, cocked his head to one side and drew smoke through the half cigar he'd placed on the curled edge of an ashtray earlier, he leaned forward and winked, "I'm listening, *blood-cousin.*"

Irish Pete drew out a plan, one that involved selling a silver mine…that is, selling it once the groundwork had been laid. The large redheaded man with bushy eyebrows and a nose that looked like it might be in competition with an apple spoke to Slats through heavy cigar smoke, "Rink is up to Prescott; he'll be gone for a couple more days…once he's back I want you to meet him. In the meantime, you and I shouldn't be seen together. Because when the time comes we'll want you to look like a man that don't have no ties in town, a total stranger."

"Alright, Pete," Slats drummed his fingers on the arm of the leather chair where he sat, "I'll leave the plannin' to you, knowing' you always figured down to the smallest details… you reckon it will it be okay if I play a little poker and maybe find me one of the town's finer ladies to pleasure myself a bit?" He looked up at Pete and grinned.

"I don't figure what I'd say about them doves would matter anyway," Pete smiled wide, "but the poker playing… well that would be all the better. You need to make it look like you got a good sized stash of cash, because that's a part of the roll we need you to play. You got plenty to work with?"

Slats rolled the cigar between his fingers and looked Pete in the eye, "I got more than twelve thousand – and mind you, I plan to build on it when I sit for poker."

During the meeting with Irish Pete, the skinny outlaw didn't mention Jimmy. This wasn't the time for it. He'd make a decision on how to bring his young partner into the fold down the road, after thing began to fall into place. Besides, after what Pete had said about it being best for Slats to look the part of a stranger in town, it would be best for Jimmy not to know more than was necessary. There wasn't no telling what Jimmy might tell a saloon girl, or anyone else for that matter. Secrets remain secrets longer when fewer people know.

It was late when Slats walked under the sign at the bottom of the stairs again. Lantern lights along the boardwalks impressed him, '*seems this town has come a long way since I was here*'. The subdued sound of a music box lifted gently from a tent down the street, the shadow of a man playing it could be seen through the dingy canvas and the pale white moon hung in the sky like a big egg. From the end of the street a woman screamed belligerent remarks carried on the wings of a cooling wind, and a pair of dogs barked back at her. The muffled sound of a slamming door followed. A dozen drunks lay propped up in doorways spewing occasional groans and snores. It was a quarter after two in the morning and Globe had settled for the night.

Slats wondered about Jimmy – hopefully he'd find him back in their room at *The Emerald*, but he wouldn't be willing to bet on it…likely he'd been separated from the money, even that in his boot!

CHAPTER THIRTEEN – JIMMIE DOSS, OUTLAW

Deputy Scoot Wilkins idled away time in the main room of the mountain cabin sitting atop a soft bearskin that covered the seat on an oversized chair fashioned from sticks of white bark aspen. Bright sunlight cascaded through the window from the side of the cabin, the light shaft alive with tiny dust particles that swam with no pattern, nor an ambition to get anywhere, only to meander slowly through the brilliance as if they knew their time was limited should they attain the near-gold square marked on the floor boards.

The interior of the cabin was still, seeming to preserve the mourning of Nato-mata-chee yesterday evening. It was quiet enough that scraping sounds from a small gray mouse that twitched from under the door could be heard between the distant occasional cries of the crows in the tall pines.

Scoot held an open book, *Homer's Odyssey*, and was reading. His lips moved but there was no sound to justify the movement. Breaking the silence within the cabin, Scoot looked over to Matt and said, "I don't know what to make of this," he nodded, "I never was one to read much." He closed the book after another glance, rose from the chair and walked across the room, placed the book on a shelf in the void between others that set in an even row four feet in length. "You think that ole boy reads these?" He tilted his head toward the porch and waved a hand across the shelf of books.

Isaiah had indeed read the collection of books. He'd read each of them several times.

When nature-loving Isaiah was a boy not more than ten years old back in Philadelphia, his father, Abraham Worsham, had been a scholar and professor of law in a college there. He saw to it that his son read, he demanded Isaiah read the classics and everything else he could find to read, even some of the law books from which he instructed. When visiting the library at the direction of his father, the youngster discovered paperbacks and dime novels depicting the western frontier and mountain men. He'd day-dreamed of being one of them, allowing his imagination to take him there, living a wild and free style of life like those he read about. But he never hinted of such a thing to his father, knowing it would only upset him, as it was so different from the life style they lived in the big city. And Professor Worsham's general description of The West depicted the population there to be basically wild and disorganized. And then the day came young Isaiah could hardly believe, his father told him they were moving to the Rocky Mountains of Colorado Territory. The boy relished the idea, exhilaration rushed through him like wild fire on a Texas prairie. But he had to keep his feelings under wraps, not to let his father know.

At the time, Isaiah didn't realize his father had contracted tuberculosis. Even if he had been told of the disease he couldn't know his father suffered and agonized with it. He wasn't a man to complain about his feelings openly. He was the sort that did a lot of listening and kept things to himself until he felt the need otherwise. He would study on the matter, and if he thought it necessary he would take action with words. That was his weapon – words! He utilized the English language with the skill of an accomplished duelist. He could perform an argument in a manner that either amazed or befuddled an adversary, lacerating an opponent with precise efficiency, and then slay him with a final oratory of perfectly chosen and well spoken words. It was said at the law school that he was Shakespeare with a law degree.

The excitement and glory of the trip was snuffed out before it could be completed. On the trail, fifty miles short of Denver, five road agents halted the small wagon train that the Worshams were a part of. Isaiah's father, being a master with phrases and logic, set about to take charge on behalf of the group of settlers; he attempted to talk the band of hooligans away from trouble. He parlayed a mixture of words into near magic, drummed down the leader of the outlaw gang like a child lost in the world, far from the hands of the Lord and set on a path toward the torments of hell. The outlaw held his gun cocked and ready all the while, but became stunned into a case of drop-jaw and blinked his eyes like a woman caught in a sand storm. The other bandits laughed and ridiculed the leader, said the old professor, dressed in his clean white shirt and city suit of clothes, cut the man into tiny pieces - did so with a sword of spirited phrases. That was when the filthy, humiliated thug, after being chastised by his cohorts, turned back toward Abraham Worsham and placed a pair of well directed balls of lead into Abraham Worsham's chest.

Professor Worsham's body was taken into town and placed in a proper cemetery. Isaiah's mother never wanted to leave Denver afterward, as her husband was buried there. She died of the fever two years later and the Worsham boy was taken in by church members. The mountains became his home from that time forward.

By the boy's fifteenth birthday he set about tracing into the majestic peaks with a group of trappers and learned to live with the wilderness. Isaiah related the story to his son, John-Eagle-Heart, telling about his mother's death, knew how he felt, said he'd never gotten over it. And he found most men never stopped missing their ma, and likely neither would he, but in time he'd learn to live with it.

Matt Ragle walked slump-shouldered to the stove and filled his coffee cup. It was right about an hour past sunup. Tomorrow morning – if Hank hadn't come around by this time tomorrow, he and Scoot would pack up and take in after the outlaws. It had been four nights and three full days. If the men they pursued got too far ahead, they might never be caught. And Matt figured there was the possibility that Hank would never come out of the coma – not likely, but possible.

"Matt," Scoot's voice echoed through the cabin, "come over here…his eyes opened, and he moved his head…like he was tryin' to figure where he was."

Matt shifted a chair to the side of the bed and pulled it up to where Hank could see him, "Well," he stared into Hank's eyes, "it's been a long time!"

Hank slowly rolled his groggy, aching head and his lips parted slightly. But the first effort to talk was useless. He cleared his throat. A rough, thick voice came, "Guess I got shot, huh?"

Matt nodded, "Yep, you took a slug on the side of your head from a Sharps long gun. Probably got yourself a concussion…almost got killed." Matt turned and motioned toward Isaiah and the boy, "You're in their cabin…in the valley we was working down to."

The light silhouetted the Worshams standing at the foot of the bed. Hank blinked them into view, "They live here?"

"Yep."

"He the one that shot me?"

"Yea, he is, name's Isaiah Worsham, and that's his son, John Eagle-Heart." Matt sniffed, took a shallow breath and went on, "The outlaws we was chasin' killed the man's wife – the boy's mother…and the two of them thought it was us that had done it, is the reason he shot ya."

The ex-Ranger raised his head for a better look, "Killed his wife? Can't say as I blame the man for shooting at us." He blinked and looked questionably at Matt, "You and Scoot okay?"

"We're fine, you're the only one that got shot."

The wounded man with the wrapping around his head put his hands to his side and pushed against the bed, attempting to rise, "Oooh! That's awful – my head's spinnin' like a Christmas top." He laid back. A grimace contorted his face and his eyes went shut.

"Dizzy, huh?" Matt dabbed a wet cloth on Hank's forehead.

Another day passed before Hank could sit on the side of the bed and sip venison soup. His hand rose to the bandage wrap. "There's still some spinnin' in there…and a bit of tenderness there on the side too." He blinked several times, "You say I been here…how long?"

"This will be the fifth day…want to try standing?" Matt mothered at the lawman uneasily.

When Hank finally got to his feet with Matt's help, it was for only a few seconds. The dizziness still owned him. Matt Ragle sat with Hank and told him the full story of the mountain man's wife, Nato-mata-chee, the Shoshone girl, and how she'd been killed.

The following morning Isaiah and the boy packed a case of dynamite and other supplies on a horse and set out for the mountainside, intending to blast away what remained of the old trail. The mountain man didn't want anybody else coming up through there. It was no longer just home, here in the valley, now it was also Nato-mata-chee's sacred ground, not to be disturbed.

Matt moved from the door down to where Isaiah and John were preparing to depart, "When Hank can travel we'll be going on. We'll first go up to Globe, and if we can keep a trail we might go on further…why don't you and your son come along with us? It'd give the youngster a chance to see a real town."

"Was there maybe a couple months back, go ever spring to supply up. John here," he gently knuckled the dark hair atop the boy's head, "knows his way around down in Globe, even got some of that stick honey last time." He looked over to the grave of Nato-tama-chee, "Can't say we like it there a lot, them folks got a different idea of what life's about." Isaiah stroked his beard and held the pipe to his lips, "We'll not be going with you'ens. You go on…if you catch up with them men, I'd be beholding' to ya if you'd let us know."

Isaiah went on to tell Matt that tying in with the lawmen wasn't a mountain way, and it wasn't the way of the Shoshone. Living in the mountains taught a man patience. There was an order for things – putting things out of order was usually trouble…and there were things a man had to do on his own if he could do it. Killin' should be more personal, not a thing for crowd-gathering.

Being a lawman, Matt wasn't sure just how he should take Isaiah's rejection. Matt didn't let it drop, "You could stay there in town for the winter and then come back here in the spring. It'd do you and the boy some good!"

"I'll do some thinkin' on it." Isaiah looped the lead rope of the packhorse over his shoulder and started toward the rise. John took up the long gun and ran on ahead. Isaiah had promised him he'd get to shoot an elk or deer if they was to see one.

113

CHAPTER FOURTEEN - JIMMY DOSS, OUTLAW

To Slats astonishment, Jimmy was in his bed at the Emerald Hotel. He was fully clothed, rumpled, and dirty, still in his boots. Slats lifted the lamp globe and lit the wick. He needed a closer look. When in arm's reach, he could see the welt along his young partner's cheek and a slight cut in the brow over a bruised eye socket. He was breathing heavy and smelled of saloon whiskey.

Rather than wake him and give him what-for, Slats decided to leave him be until morning. He figured Jimmy was too drunk to make much sense anyhow. And those marks on his face were sure to have a story behind them. That too would wait.

The lanky man undressed and slipped quietly into his bed. In no time he was making bizarre sounds that would make a hibernating bear blink and scratch.

Slats rolled his lean body toward the gray light of morning that whispered through the window around the curtain. It had been a short night but one that wasn't wasted by the Irishman. He stretched his long arms and shook his body awake. The bed was the first he'd slept in for over three weeks and the ground's morning chill wasn't missed.

Jimmy was flat on his back. He rasped out snorting noises that might be confused with slopping of the hogs back in Missouri. *'That boy could sleep on a cactus in the midst of a snowstorm,'* the slinky Irishman thought to himself. Slats pulled on his pants and stuck one long arm into a shirtsleeve when a dainty, *tap, tap, tap* sounded at the door. He listened dubiously, wondering for sure what he'd heard. *Tap, tap, tap!* This time this very feminine voice accompanied the tapping.

"Jimmy? You in there, Jimmy?"

"Just a minute," Slats answered as he buttoned his canvas pants and buckled his belt. Both arms were in his shirt but it remained unbuttoned when he reached the door. He tilted his head toward the doorframe, careful not to stand directly in front of it. "What do you want?" He asked the question trying to sound more like Jimmy than himself.

"Jimmy, it's me, Lillian."

With revolver in hand, Slats jerked the door open. He looked over the head of a frail young lady and scrutinized the hallway. He stepped back and gave her a brief once-over. She was dressed like one of the dancing girls the man had seen many times before in the saloons and dance halls. Only this girl was much prettier than most.

When she first eyed the gun and caught a ready view of the tall spindly man she gasped and jerked both hands to her rose colored lips. The jolting initial surprise lapsed readily and she softened into a dainty, loveable character, a pose she found easy to assume.

Long blond curls draped her face and were held in place by pink ribbons. "Oh, I'm sorry." The girl rose to her tiptoes and tried to look past Slat's arm, looking for the room number on the door, "I thought this was Jimmy's room!"

"He's still asleep," Slats drew back from the door and motioned with his head for the girl to look inside. She leaned and stared into the stillness, darkness still held somewhat against the new light of morning. Jimmy hadn't moved.

"Is he alright?" She looked up into Slats' face and then, stepping back, she gauged him completely from head to his bare feet. Her eyes timidly related the soft, sweet words Slats had seen and heard many times, especially in his younger years, "Hello, mister."

Slats nodded and smiled.

"He helped me last night," the girl spoke softly, "and I was hoping to thank him again…and see if he was badly hurt."

"Somebody whooped him did they?" Slats grinned as he stepped backward into the room.

She followed.

He sat on the bed and bent to pull his boots on.

"Oh, Jimmy won the fight!" Her eyes sparkled as she said it. "He wrestled the knife away from the other man and knocked him to the floor several times before it ended with Jimmy up and hittin' the man on the noggin with his gun… that done him in." Lillian shook her head in an affirmative motion, giving perky action to the curls teeming about her lovely face, "Yep, done knocked him down for good."

Slats sprang to his feet, startled and fidgety, "You mean it killed him?"

"No. It didn't kill him," she hesitated with a frown, "knocked him into the middle of next week though, I reckon." Looking down at Jimmy, the young woman clasped her hands together at her bosom and said, "When he wakes up will you please tell him I was here…I'm Lillian," she waited to be positive Slats had understood the name, "to thank him, and see how he was." She blinked, awaiting Slats' answer.

The tall outlaw scratched at his ear. With a twist of his head, looking at Jimmy, he said, "Shore, I'll tell him. Lillian, huh?"

"That's correct, sir, and you are…?"

"Friends call me Slats." Remembering the conversation of the previous night with Pete, Slats thought a bit more of an explanation might be well placed at this point. "Until a month ago I was the co-owner of a silver mine in Tombstone…you know where that is?"

"Well, yes, everybody's heard of Tombstone."

"I sold my holdings there and figured maybe I'd see what this part of the country had to offer. I'd been told some of the richest silver ore in the world is holdin' in the mountains here."

"Oh, you and Jimmy are friends, huh?" Her enticing charm moved up a notch.

"Well…he works for me." Slats shook his head up and down three or four times and continued, "He don't know much about mining and such, but he's a good man to go fetch things…keeps me in cigars, and acts as my body guard." The tall outlaw tilted his head toward Jimmy's bed, "You saw him, the man can fight when need be."

"He sure enough can do that." She smiled daintily, "You will be sure and tell him?"

"That I will – first thing when he comes outta that deep sleep."

"Very good, Mr. Slats. I guess I'll go on for now," she turned to leave, "and if you would, please tell him to call on me sometime today…or tonight."

"I'll do that…by the way, miss, can you tell me where I could find a tailor shop here in town. The valise with all my regular clothes was lost somewhere along the stage route and I'll be in need of a couple of suits of clothes right soon."

"Why I certainly can, sir. Up the street a ways, on the next street over, there's a shop called Bong-Lo's Tailors. They do very handsome work there, I'm sure you'd be pleased."

Lillian shuffled out the door and down the hall to the top of the staircase. Slats leaned on the doorframe watching. She looked back, turned and waved the fingers of her petite hand orderly, like playing a piano, "Be sure and tell Jimmy I was here," her melodious voice chimed.

The stout, spindly man pushed the door shut and walked to the bed. Jimmy continued with the ludicrous snoring, undisturbed by the conversation in the room. Slats gathered a fist full of the blanket that lay under the placid blond man and jerked it like a cowboy bulldogging a steer. Ready or not, the day was beginning for the boy that won a fight the prior night, even if he looked like he'd been the loser.

Slats tended to the boy's wound and told him of the visit by Lillian. The crooked smile Jimmy evoked displayed satisfaction of Lillian's concern about him. With a show of pride he related his side of the fight. Slats dabbed at the abrasion with a whiskey soaked cloth. "So Lillian and one of the barkeeps toted you back to *The Emerald*…I don't

suppose that's going to keep you from going back to the...
what'd you call it, the Gemstone Dance Hall.?"

"There you go again, pappyin' me. That girl took a
liking to me...I reckon I'll drop by and thank her for
askin' about me this morning. I don't see no harm in being
gentlemanly."

Within the hour the two of them took themselves a
hearty breakfast in the hotel dining room.

Other folks took second looks; Jimmy's eye, battered
cheek and brow, left no doubt in the mind of anyone that
laid eyes on him that he had been in a scrape with a worthy
opponent.

"I ain't going to ask you not to go see her...you wouldn't
listen anyhow, but you got to let up on that whiskey, you
gotta promise me that."

Jimmy held his coffee cup steady at his lips and looked
over the top into Slats' eyes but didn't answer for a minute.

"You can't drink too much like you did last night – I'm
not putting up with it...and you can see what it got you.
You're lucky that fellow didn't carve you up...between him
and that Indian girl, you don't seem to have too much luck
with people with knives."

Jimmy threw the remark off with a snarled lip and flip
of his head.

Slats told his young partner about the meeting he had
with Pete, "I suppose you can see that I can't be lookin' after

you like you was my kid or somethin'.'" After another sip of coffee and a nasty glare, Slats said, "Did ya fork out all that money ya had?"

The sheepish gaze dropped off the youngster's face momentarily. With his chin raised defiantly he quipped an answer, "Nope, still got most of it – never took off my boots either."

"Humph," the skinny man responded, and added, "you stay out of fights, boy. You get yourself in more trouble like you did last night and not only will you be out of the big money plans, you might find yourself at the bottom of a mine shaft." The tall outlaw was tougher on Jimmy than need be over something as trivial as a fight, but he wanted to make the impression that he needed the boy to steer clear of trouble.

Slats paid for breakfast and handed the waitress an extra silver dollar. They exited the hotel and stood on the boardwalk out front. He lit another of the five cent cigars and said to Jimmy through a small cloud of unfamiliar smelling smoke, "I'm headed over to Bong Lo's. I'm getting me some suits of clothes made, like I told ya, I've got to play the part of a well-to-do man, and I'm gonna do it right. There's big money to be made." He emphasized the 'big money' and pointed the end of the fresh chewed cigar toward Jimmy. "You keep your boots clean and your face outta fights if you wanta be rich one day soon."

CHAPTER FIFTEEN – JIMMY DOSS, OUTLAW

For the next three days Slats played a lot of poker, straight up, honest poker! He wasn't new to the game being played legitimate; it just took longer to move the money into his hands than in his usual manner of play. He tossed cash around like there was no limit to his bankroll. And he took reasonable opportunities to expand on his fallacious story of ownership in the silver mine in Tombstone that he'd created first with Jimmy's gal, Lillian.

Jimmy mostly kept an eye on Slats. He stayed nearby, playing the role that his outlaw partner bequeathed upon him. But he'd disappear for an hour each afternoon, and again later in the evening, usually getting back to his 'Slats-duty' by midnight. It wasn't spoken between them but there was no doubt– Lillian was the reason.

Having generated a name for himself as a poker player, Slats began to frequent *The Royal,* the saloon and gambling hall adjacent to his cousin's loan office, owned by Irish Pete's friend, Rick Slater. More than once Pete stood at a distance and watched Slats perform at the tables, and he hadn't missed the fact that a young man also seemed to have his eyes on the skinny Irishman. He wondered if there was something that Slats hadn't told him that night in his office.

And then one evening Irish Pete ambled over to the table where Slats had gathered together sizeable winnings. He tapped the shoulder of a well-dressed, white haired gentleman sitting directly across the table from Slats. The man turned abruptly and looked up at Pete. The scowl on his face melted into an amiable facade before he turned back to the game. When it came his turn to bet he threw his cards face down in the middle of the table, "I'm out! Seems I can't get any kind of luck but the bad kind." With those words he gathered his dwindled stack of legal tender and rose, "Thank you, gentlemen, for a fine evening."

Pete scooted back the vacated chair, seated himself and extracted a roll of currency from his inside coat pocket. "No such thing as a bad-luck-chair that sits this good…maybe a bad poker player, wouldn't you say mister?" He looked into his cousin's eyes across the table and smiled.

"Mister, if you got that kind of money," Slats studied the stack of bills Pete placed on the table in from of him, "I'm just right happy to have you come aboard."

"New in town, Mr. Long-Drink-Of-Water?" Irish Pete chided. It was a phrase he'd occasionally used to identify Slats when they were younger, back east.

"Yes, sir I am…new in town, that is." Slats shuffled the cards and looked at Irish Pete over the plume of cigar smoke he blew in his direction, "How about you? You a citizen of this town, or just come here to pass your money off to me?"

The two men, cousins by the blood of their mothers, played their roles. Others at the table had no idea. Talk between the men aroused interests with more than a few of the saloon's patrons. A game with high stakes and an exchange of crisp remarks between the two men that dominated both the conversation and the winnings was more entertaining than songs sung off-key by a worn out dove and a half-drunk piano player.

- -

A week passed. Hank Darcy had made little notable progress. His strength was returning but the dizziness blunted his actions. There were times he couldn't keep his eyes focused and needed to steady himself with a hand on a chair back or door frame.

Hank didn't argue when Matt and Scoot reprimanded him for trying to accomplish things within the cabin he wasn't yet capable of doing. But he became near violent when he surmised they debated whether to go on without him. "No, by damn, you ain't going! This is something I have to do and you ain't doing it without me." Hank got so worked up it worried Matt, made him think Hank might go into a full blown stroke. He couldn't let that happen. And Hank kept saying, "Just a couple more days, that's all…just a couple more days and I'll be shut of this."

The blasting of the mountainside by Isaiah and the boy lasted two and a half days. Isaiah made sure this time. There'd be no more people make their way up that old trail. Even the elk and deer might have to find a new trail to the summer grass in the high lands; the old pathway was absolutely gone, obliterated.

The mountain man and the Indian boy brought a young spike buck to the cabin when they returned. John Eagle-Heart had shot it. "A clean lung shot," bragged Isaiah, "from well over a hundred and fifty yards." Pride showed in the voluminous man.

There was no shortage of food. An elk hindquarter, three wild hog hams, slabs of bacon and venison jerky hung in the smoking shed. The better part of a fifty pound bag of beans and three dozen cans of fruit sat in the corner along with the flour and coffee dumped on the floor by Slats which was mostly saved.

It was the eighth day after Hank took the bullet to the side of his head. He worked his way out the door and onto the porch. Matt stood nearby, watching. The ex-Ranger, noticing the grave of Nato-mata-chee, looked over to Matt, "That where the boy's mother is buried?"

"Yep, that's it."

"What's the bell for?"

"The man and boy say that's so the bell will ring out to The Great Spirit to come and fetch her up," Matt hesitated, "to keep her spirit from the evils of the white man."

Hank blinked his eyes in a manner that Matt could tell he was to ward off dizziness. Afterward, he spoke with a strange softness in his voice, "I always wondered why our kind is so ornery and mean. Some men kill innocent folks with no real purpose, for most anything – they kill for money, for land…or whatever." He shrugged his broad shoulders, "Seems to me men kill just to be killing." He looked up into the mountains, "What if all species, not just man, killed like that?" He stumbled and caught himself against a porch roof support post, "And we're supposed to be the ones with the best brains…God's choice above all creatures." When he shook his head this time it wasn't to clear dizziness.

"I got fresh coffee inside, Hank."

"Just a couple more days," Hank spoke under his breath as he methodically turned to go inside.

- -

High stakes poker with Slats and Pete dominating had become a regular evening event at *The Royal.* The two of them generally relieved the others of their money before the night ended.

To the unknowing regulars who gathered in the saloon it appeared the two copious poker-playing-gentlemen maintained a type of friendly hostility between them.

Some of the town's well-to-do, business men and mine owners frequented poker nights with *the loud mouth redhead,* and *the skinny rich man.* Word was out...poker had rarely been played in Globe like it was being played now! Big money poker had become an attraction.

Carlton Claypool, the sole owner of the Resolution Mine, which was claimed to be the highest-grade ore in the Globe area, found his way to *The Royal* and Pete and Slats' table.

"Claypool...I've heard of you." Irish Pete Murray rolled back and forth in his chair as he methodically made the statement. With his cigar raised in salute, he went on, "Welcome, Mr. Claypool." With that, he took up the deck of cards, held them in his left hand and began introducing others around the table, pointing nonchalantly with the chewed end of the dark cigar loosely held in the right, "This here is Al Hollings," Pete nodded at the man with streaked brown and white hair and a baroque moustache sitting next to him. He continued orderly, calling out names as he shuffled the cars. "That there is Cooper Winfrey, he owns the mercantile and grocery. Next across from me is Kendrick McClary," Pete grinned wide, "you probably heard of him… used to own a mine down in Tombstone." Each of the men either nodded or looked up at Claypool as their name was spoken. And Pete could tell as he hastily studied their faces, no one questioned the fictitious statement about Slats' ownership of a silver mine, until Claypool.

"Mr. McClary…, humm, don't think I know the name, but then nobody knows all the folks that own mines in Arizona Territory." He grinned a callous grin and his attention quickly diverted to the cards being dealt as he feathered a noteworthy stack of crisp bills onto the table.

There were no big losers this night. There were, however, two big winners – the cousins, Pete and Slats. They had maneuvered the man into their game that Irish Pete Murray had set his sights on, Carlton Claypool!

Pete secretly was able to get a note to Slats as the game ended just after midnight.

Come to my office in the morning.
The fruit is ripe for picking.

The following morning, in Pete's office, a cigar odor cloud hung in the air like the room was readied to cure fresh-hung meat. Irish Pete waved his hands extensively; his large forearms thoroughly covered with bushy rust colored hair, took on the appearance of fledging stalks of saguaro cactus. And the two cousins couldn't have been more arrogant if they were a couple of crooked politicians who had just bought an election, and with it, control of the town.

"Here, Kendrick, have another." Pete poured a tall glass of rye whiskey for Slats and then clinked the bottle on his own glass once again. "By glory, skinny man, you played the role like a well-oiled stage actor." He threw a large open palm in the air, "I figured you for good, boy, but I didn't know you could be that damn good!" Pete laughed and shook his head emphatically as he exhaled another billow of gray-white smoke.

"I always knew I should ought'a be a rich man," Slats wide smile showed pride, "and you," he pointed a long finger at Pete, "had them fellas eatin' outta the palm of your hand like little birds in a nest sucking' worms from mommy's mouth...you was somethin' to behold." The two of them giggled like a pair of schoolboys who'd just stolen a watermelon.

"You reckon our mommas would be proud of us?" Pete stared into Slats' eyes, seemingly with earnest, then clapped his big hands together and sucked in a breath, "Whooee... what have we gone and done?" His laughter grew louder, and Slats slapped himself on the knee three times in rapid succession, laughing and coughing.

Finally, after they'd calmed down a bit, Pete said, "Here…not much left in this bottle, let's just finish this off and I'll lay out the plan for you, cousin."

CHAPTER SIXTEEN -
JIMMY DOSS, OUTLAW

Irish Pete's expression grew somber. The business of selling a silver mine where maybe a half million dollars could be at stake, wasn't something to be taken lightly. And the manner in which his plan called for the money to change hands could get a man killed. If the people that lost that kind of money didn't do the killing, the law in a silver-controlled town would likely consider hanging to be a proper punishment.

The big redhead had lived most of his life as if it was a game to rid others of their money. Even as a boy he'd been bigger than most of kids his age. And they were aware that Pete would take their pennies from them if he knew they had any. The owners of local stores kept a wary eye open if ornery Pete was in his store, especially if the boy was near candy jars.

When grown and out in the world on his own Irish Pete Murray never stayed long in one place. It was often the only way he could avoid the law or the people he'd bilked out of their bankroll. He'd never killed anyone, nor had he ever stolen enough money to have his name on a dodger, but he always left very mad people looking toward the end of town he rode away from. He'd spent a good portion of his years moving around after leaving the big cities back east. He really didn't like Arizona all that much; it was just that no one knew him there. And he had indeed changed his ways somewhat since his arrival in Globe. He'd made a brief, ineffectual effort to make a near-honest living, although there were consistently those that weren't comfortable about the loan office he ran. His loan business was small scale, usually not more than a few hundred dollars. The pompous life he led was supported mostly by a deck of cards. He'd never compiled enough honest capital otherwise.

Pete moved a few papers and slid a lamp to the side of his desk. He then lifted a map from a desk drawer and spread it across the open space he'd arranged. "I own me a couple of small diggings here in town – and I'd just come to be the owner of a mine there," Pete placed a finger on the map indicating a spot less than a mile up the valley, north of town, "that's when I sent you that letter." Pete stood erect and placed his hands on his hips, "I made a loan to a man who'd come from Ohio with more grit in his jaw than money in his pocket. He struck a pretty good vein of ore, enough so that every man-jack in Globe knew he'd done it."

"So how'd you come to get his mine?" Slats figured on something a step or two outside of total honesty had taken place. He looked at Pete out of the corner of his eye and a wink disclosed his thoughts.

"No, no, no…weren't no dirty dealing took place at all." Pete leaned forward, looking back at the map, "Everybody in town knew I'd loaned the man some money, enough to get him some heavier equipment and hire on some men. Nothing but a straight out deal – this one had no babble in it."

"So what happened?"

"Well, one of his diggers, at least that's what we all figured, killed him…put a shovel to his neck sideways, nearly cut his head clean off. That son-of-a-bitch run off with the money I'd loaned Johnson and cleared out of the territory." After two or three abbreviated puffs on his cigar, Pete went on, "By all rights, even according to the law, I became the rightful owner of that mine when the loan couldn't be paid."

Slats raised his eyebrows and hunched his shoulders, "So…we're going into the mining business?"

"For a spell…but just for a spell. You see, we're fixin' to sell that mine to Claypool. Pete sat back in his tufted leather chair and put a foot on the edge of the desk. "I've got another mine owner that owes me on a loan I made to him. He's got a right good piece of action goin', maybe not for long, but for now he's pulling some high-grade stuff outta his hole. His loan is due come Friday and he ain't got time to get his silver milled out and turned to cash, so he wants to pay me with three wagons of ore. I figure, by his assay, that it'll bring more than what he owes, so I'm willing to take it."

"Sounds like you got yourself a good deal alright," Slats gave Pete a queried look, "and how was I fittin' into the picture?"

"This here ore is being delivered in payment – he's bringin' it over to the Johnson mine – the one I showed you on the map. Talk about the luck of the Irish," Pete chuckled. "What I'd intended before this came to us like a gift from glory, was to have you buy three to four thousand dollars worth of ore…and with that we was going to pull the same jiggery-pokery, but with your money." Pete's grin seemed to soften his big nose into a mushroom, "But don't you worry, cousin, I got plans for you money, you ain't getting off that easy."

"I don't get it yet, Pete, how's that make you and me rich?"

"Keep yer pants on, Kendrick, I'm getting to that."

"Okay, okay, so get to it if ya don't mind."

The red headed Irishman poured another glass of rye whiskey, taking his time, knowing he was tinkering with his bony cousin, same as he did when they were boys. "Well, I got the word out to the right places, mostly to Claypool, that I've got that ole mine back in operation. Tomorrow I'm going to ask him to have one of his engineers take a look at my three wagons of ore sitting there in the mouth of the mine and tell me if I really got me somethin' or if I'm just wasting time and money to keep diggin'."

"You are a slick ole snake, Pete."

"I'm also going to let Claypool know you've made me a pretty fair offer on my mine. He already knows I don't know much about mining," Pete lifted his shoulders and reared back, "so I'm looking like a limp-necked chicken ready for the pluckin'."

"So, now about my bankroll?"

"Okay…Claypool is coming tonight to sit in on our poker game again. When the time is right, and you'll know by what I say at the table, you're gonna pull ten thousand dollars out and say, "Oh, by the way, Mr. Murray…it'd look all the better for you to call me mister," Pete winked, "here's the ten thousand down money on that mine we talked about. And of course I'll take it up and put it in my pocket."

Slats sat quiet. He chewed and digested the information Irish Pete put on his plate. The plan seemed to be solid enough. He rekindled his remembrance of Carlton Claypool, *'Could Claypool be tricked…after all, it was his backyard the game was being played in.'*

"I've got this figured to where Claypool could offer up to four to five hundred thousand for that mine. I don't know want no tom-foolery to get in the way." Pete leaned back, kept his hand to his mouth and puffed the cigar held between his thumb and forefinger. His eyes riveted on Slats long thin face, "Just one more thing, Cousin Kendrick, don't you think it's time you told me about that boy that keeps his eye on you like you was a mouse and he's a big ol' barn owl?"

Slats squirmed and wrinkled his mouth before any words came. "He ain't no problem for you to worry with," he stretched his long legs out in front of him, leaned back in the chair and gathered his thoughts, "He rode with me on a bank job…handled himself real good, but he's not of the right stuff for me to keep around; I'm fixing to get rid of him."

"Wait a minute, cuz, we can't have no killin – could be some other folks about town have seen the boy with his eye on you same as I have. This ain't no time to take risks."

Slats came forward in the chair, "No, nothin' like that; I got me a plan, one that won't be no obstacle…fact is I kind of like the boy, but I can get rid of him without killin'." He rubbed both hands on his thighs, "I'll be settin' my plan in motion likely tomorrow…don't you be worrying about it…I give my word on my mother's grave."

The poker game with Claypool, including the charade with ten thousand dollars went as planned by the Irish cousins. On queue Slats lifted ten thousand dollars onto the table and pushed it over in front of Pete. "Here's the down payment, Mr. Murray…I guess you'll be getting' me the papers sometimes in the week?"

"Got 'em all in my safe," Pete smirked.

Carlton Claypool's eyes lit up like the burst of a rocket on the fourth of July when the money changed hands. Anybody paying any attention at all could see his mind clattering like gold being dumped into a treasure chest by a patch-eye-pirate.

The prodigious mine owner insensibly fingered the cards he'd been dealt. As he arranged them in his hand he studied the faces of Pete and Kendrick who pulled off the showy money exchange with the precision of a magic act. Others at the table reflected on the event with lifted eyebrows or peered at the malicious twosome from the corner or an eye. There were a few onlookers, feeling they were witnessing a noteworthy exchange of a sizeable enterprise – Claypool saw the gawks also…he wasn't accustom to being second fiddle in financial matters.

"It's your bet, Mr. Claypool." Pete Murray's voice was like an alarm clock to the explicitly dressed middle-aged man. He quickly fanned his cards and slid one from the middle of the five over to the side, a totally novice move for a competent poker player. "I'll open for ten thou…ummph, I mean ten dollars," he placed a blue chip in the center of the table.

Slats fingered a stack of currency and pulled out five twenty dollar bills, "Well I feel right lucky; let's make it a hundred."

Al Hollings fiddled with his moustache and mumbled, "I'll call that," and he casually pushed a pile of red chips into the stack of currency that Slats bet.

Claypool responded when the players looked at him, his turn having come to call the raise, "I know when I'm bested." He tossed his cards face down toward the dealer, "But just because I'm down with one hand doesn't mean I'm out of the game." He stared coldly at Irish Pete, "I always stick around…sometimes it's difficult to determine whose going to be the big winner when the game is just getting under way."

Irish Pete was right proud of himself. When he'd requested Claypool to examine his loads of ore, there was an insinuation that his deal with the tall rich man, McClary, hadn't been consummated. He could tell by the rich mine owner's poorly suited poker-face that he would come ready to call – or raise. The amount, Pete figured, would depend on the engineer's analysis of the ore; but if it was less than two hundred and fifty thousand, Pete would play a bluff hand.

CHAPTER SEVENTEEN – JIMMY DOSS, OUTLAW

The chill of morning had slipped out of the mountain pass, pushed by the gentle breeze that fingered the trees and ushered in the sun from behind the mountaintops.

Irish Pete stood at the mine's entrance. Anxiety flirted with him. Two days earlier he'd hired a couple of no-accounts from saloons to work the mine, knowing they'd not do much except lean on a shovel. But that's all he wanted from them.

He brought another man with him this morning, a mid-aged fellow who was dressed in well pressed trousers, white shirt, dark brown coat and string tie. The man was new in town but a friend of Rick Slater, proprietor of *The Royal*. His past was tainted, but he knew his way around mining and could figure ore content with the best of them. Pete Murray was counting on that.

The big redhead saw in the distance a contingent of riders coming up the grade toward him.

Claypool rode a big white horse, *'must be seventeen hands'*, Pete thought. *Wonder why he didn't come in that rig with the padded leather seat he trots around in?'* Three men rode with him, one in front and two behind. The two bringing up the rear carried Winchesters across the pommels and had pistols strapped down to their thighs. It appeared they were there to insure the safety of the owner of the Revolution Mine. *'Or was there more to their presence than safety?'* Pete wondered.

He stood and watched the approaching men. "Morning, Mr. Claypool," Pete shouted when the four riders were within distance. When they were reining in their mounts and close enough to hear, Pete turned to his two roustabout-miners with shovels, "You two…take the day off! Git on outta here…find yourself a lady friend to rest up with…and be back here tomorrow morning at the regular time or I'll have the both of you replaced with one good Irishman." He grinned wide and chuckled.

"It's hard to keep good ones, huh?" Claypool half-chuckled as he stepped down. He rubbed the kidney areas of his back with both of his hands, "I'm not accustomed to the saddle, but there are times when a man has to make sacrifices for a friend, wouldn't you say, Mr. Murray?"

"Yes sir! My father taught me that when I was just a wee little tyke…taught me with a switch, he did, so's I'd not forget."

Claypool gave Pete a sideward glance, "No since in wasting away the day. With the flip of his wrist he indicated a slight-framed man wearing wire rimmed speckles, a black derby hat and flat-heeled, lace up shoes, "Mr. Murray, this is Rupert Conrad, he's my chief engineer. He can assay this ore for you better with the naked eye than most men can with chemicals…however, he brought chemicals along. I'm sure you want this to be thorough." He looked square at Pete, who didn't have an ounce of back-down in his face.

"Let's do that one first, Rupert," Claypool pointed to the wagon that was last in line of the three.

"As good a place to start as any," Pete nodded approval.

The engineer untied a satchel from atop the saddlebags on the roan he had ridden to the mine, placed it on the ground and extracted packet of objects including a bottle of dark liquid and three small metal tools.

"You want us to unload it, sir?" One of the riflemen asked.

"We don't want to make a mess of Mr. Murray's wagon, and it would take a good deal of time to shovel the ore out."

He looked at Irish Pete with a contemptuous glare, "You do want us to be as accurate as possible though, don't you, Mr. Murray?"

"Accurate? Certainly, and if you want to unload it, that's fine...those two no-accounts will be back here in the morning, it'll give them a good start on the day to shovel it back in." He was as cooperative as possible, but he ached inside, not knowing just what to expect...*was the ore up to the grade the man who owed him had represented it to be?* He hitched a brow and looked passively at Claypool, "Do as you think best."

The man in the white shirt and brown coat, the man that Pete brought with him, stepped back from having made a casual inspection of the ore in the two front wagons. He had a light benevolent smile, but one that questioned the actions he was witnessing, "Mr. Murray, this is high grade stuff." His hushed voice was matter-of-fact. Pete's brow lifted and his lips displayed a guarded grin.

Claypool and his engineer heard what was said. They exchanged a circumspect look between them as the engineer lifted another chunk of ore from the wagon. He continued his examination distant from Pete's watch and apparent indifference, but also with the close scrutiny of his boss standing nearby in his expensive, light gray, tailored suit.

"Well you and I know that," Pete asserted passively to his man, "but I've asked Mr. Claypool for his assessment – two assessments are better than one." He chuckled apologetically, and when Claypool's men weren't looking, he gripped the man by the top of his shoulder, "We'll just stand aside and let these men do what I'd asked." He squeezed and got his message across.

Jimmy Doss looked into Lilly's eyes as he twisted a curl of her hair atop the pillow, "Honey, you've done made my life worthwhile." He took a deep breath and rolled over to lie on his back next to her. Jimmy looked up at the ceiling and momentarily studied the glimmering chandelier that caught and reflected the glow of candles from the tabletop next to the bed. "Less than a month ago I was down and out in El Paso, sittin' in a saloon and wondering how I was gonna get my next meal."

"Oh, you poor dear," Lilly pressed her face against his cheek. The sorrow in her voice was genuine.

"It ain't that way no more." Jimmy remained relaxed, lying on his back he drew his hands up to just below his chest, "now I got money," he grinned, "got me a pretty woman, and ain't been hungry for nothin' for a long time." He spoke quietly, his words subdued and drawn out as if he was deep in thought.

Suddenly he bolted upright and sat cross-legged on the bed, still in his long-johns. Looking down at Lillian's face encircled in curls, he near shouted, "Why don't we get ourselves married?" His eyes were like saucers and his teeth exposed through a giant boyish grin.

Lilly lay quiet for a moment, her eyes moved in a slow, continuous motion, taking in everything all about her and Jimmy. Doubt and confusion shadowed her face in the flickering candlelight.

She drawled, "I don't know, Jimmy…that's something I'd need some time to dwell on." She turned her head toward him. The pillow pushed the long blond curls all about her face like golden puffs of clouds. "I'm kinda indebted to Linda…and she's become like a momma to me."

"What do you mean?" Jimmy's tone showed a hint of anger.

"I'm saying Linda Russell, who owns this here dance hall, she took me in when I was near dead with the fever – weren't nobody else would even come near me, let alone help me. Well she cared for me, took me into her home and saw me through the fever. Then she fed me, bought me clothes and gave me this job." Lillian was sitting up now, her legs hanging over the side of the bed, pulling her clothes on. "I promised her, Jimmy." She shook her head and fingered her hair into place as she spoke, "I promised her I'd stay here for all she's done for me."

"Promised her…for how long?"

"Well I don't know…" Lillian looked forlorn as she adjusted her skirt and blouse, "not forever…nothin's forever."

Jimmy stood and lifted his clothes from the floor, quickly buckled his britches and began pulling on his boots. Lillian walked to the dresser and sat lightly, and very femininely, on the tufted stool in front of the mirror, picked up the brush and began stroking her hair, some frustration showing. She watched him in the mirror, seeing his lips tighten.

Jimmy buttoned his shirt as he crossed the room to where Lillian sat. Dejection was apparent, but he also had the feeling that he had taken too much liberty...too soon. "We don't have to be married today, maybe we should think about it like you said." He stood behind her and gazed at her face in the mirror as she continued stroking the brush through her hair.

A tear came to the corner of Lilly's eye and she tucked her bottom lip between her teeth, but she didn't talk. She was afraid that if she tried she'd begin sobbing.

Jimmy saw her in the mirror, "I could talk with Miss Russell," he said it like it was half fact and half question.

Lillian stopped brushing, stood, turned and wrapped her arms around his neck. She leaned her head back and said very softly across adoring lips, "Jimmy Doss, you are one real dandy! It's just not the time to talk of marriage... maybe later, maybe before winter sets in." She switched her thoughts to Miss Russell, *'Nothing is forever'*.

The young outlaw's mind etched out thoughts of Slats... and Irish Pete. He thought he might not be around until winter, depending on what Slats was working on. He realized that he hadn't considered Slats and the *big money deal* he'd planned on being a part of…maybe it was a good thing Lilly didn't jump on the idea of marriage, not right away.

Carlton Claypool stood with his mine engineer and the two bodyguards, their heads close enough that their hat brims were almost touching. The conversation they had was very hushed. All eyes were on the mine engineer and the small tablet he held, staring at page after page. He seemed to be reading to Claypool from it. After what seemed to be a lifetime to Irish Pete, the exceedingly well dressed mine owner motioned toward the horses. One of the men with a rifle walked to the big white horse that was Claypool's, lifted the saddlebags and returned to the gathering with the leather bags. He handed them to his boss, stepped back and shucked a bullet into the chamber of the Winchester. The other rifleman did the same.

"Over here, Mr. Murray…come over here if you will, please.' He waved in a friendly nature; a smile seemed to be forced from his lips.

Irish Pete had been in a lot of tight spots in his life. He'd faced death more than once, been shot at – but never hit. This didn't seem to him to be that sort of situation… there was no need to summon him closer if they intended to kill him...and Irish Pete had a gut feeling about those saddlebags!

"Yes sir, Mr. Claypool, I hope your man can confirm what I'm of a mind to feel about this silver mine." The stout Irishman moved to where he'd been summoned, trying to appear confident.

"There's one hundred and fifty thousand dollars in this saddlebag." Claypool unbuckled and lifted one of the flaps, showing its' contents to Pete but sheltering it from the others.

The boisterous Irish redhead hadn't fully prepared himself for something like this – that kind of money right out, this morning. He pushed the brim of his hat back, "Well...I don't know...is what your telling me is that you want to buy my mine? Is that what this is about?" Pete tried to look surprised and somewhat reserved, in a negative sort of way.

"You're damn right that's what this is all about." Claypool stood a bit taller and pushed out his chest, "But this hundred and fifty thousand is only part of what I'm offering. There'll be another hundred thousand delivered tomorrow, when you sign the deed and claim over to me."

"I don't want to seem unappreciative, Mr. Claypool." Pete dropped his head and cut his eyes over to the wagon loads of ore. "What about Kendrick McClary, I do sort of have a deal with him...he's given me deposit money...ten thousand dollars. And even if I could get him to back off… I believe your offer is a little short of what it would take to make me break my word."

"Ten thousand, that's small potatoes. He couldn't be a serious buyer with only ten thousand dollars," Claypool frowned. He rubbed his chin and looked over to his engineer. The man made an abbreviated nod. "Tell you what, I'll pay you two hundred and eighty thousand…and throw in another twenty thousand for you to give to McClary. That should make the deal – he'd have a nice profit and there's more for you." He hesitated as Irish Pete munched his lips. The Resolution Mine owner then took on a look of hostility, "If that don't work, maybe I can have my men pay him a visit that will convince him to back off."

Irish Pete glowed inside; he'd done such a good job of working the rich man. But he also knew he'd have to clear out of Globe, out of Arizona Territory, faster than a jackrabbit that had just stumbled into a coyote's den. "You've convinced me, Mr. Claypool. That skinny card player will just have to take twenty thousand; like you say… any man that can't be glad to double his money… making ten thousand profit likely couldn't be pleased unless he was hung with a brand new rope." Pete laughed and extended his hand, "looks like we got us a deal."

Claypool barely grinned, but he extended his hand and the two men shook. "I'll be getting with you tomorrow afternoon. I'll send a man with a message in the morning. You be sure you bring that mine deed and," he paused, "listen Pete, let's make this a clean deal, I don't want no surprises, if you know what I mean."

CHAPTER EIGHTEEN –
JIMMY DOSS, OUTLAW

Isaiah and his son stood alongside and watched as Hank, Matt and Scoot saddled their horses and tied bedrolls and gear on behind. The half-Indian boy took his father's hand, looked up at him wide-eyed, "We going with 'em, Pa?"

"No, son, we'll let them go on like they're fixin' to do." The mountain man bent down and placed his hand on the boy's shoulder and said quietly, "But we won't be far behind." He winked at the boy.

Hank wrapped the cinch strap tight and dropped the stirrup into place. He rechecked the bedroll and stowed gear. The ex-Ranger shielded his eyes against the sun, checking the time, as he began a short walk to where the man stood with the boy, "Isaiah, I can't thank you enough for your hospitality…you too, John." He placed a hand on the boy's head, "I'm going to catch those men that killed your Ma, son, and they'll answer for what they done."

"Sorry I put that bullet to your head, Mr. Darcy," Isaiah Worsham said, "sure glad it didn't do you in."

"Well I'm just about as good as new. I don't reckon that bullet was intended to be the end for me. I've still got a job to do…you sure you won't come with us?"

"Nope. The boy and me, we got our own bear to skin. Now that his ma's gone, I've to look out for him by myself…but you can't tell, maybe we'll run into each other on another mountain some time." Once again Isaiah turned and winked at John.

- -

Irish Pete tried not to hurry; he didn't want to appear anxious following the eventful meeting with Carlton Claypool. He rode to the livery rather than directly back to his office.

The ride back to town from the mine gave the Irishman more time to think. If Claypool was having him watched, wouldn't it be appropriate to place that kind of money in the bank for safekeeping! He placed the saddlebags over his arm and walked straight-away to the bank, all the while telling himself to keep calm and collected. He hesitated on the boards three or four feet short of the entryway, looked all about, patted the bags and stepped forward.

Pete methodically pushed the heavy door shut behind him and strolled through the short banister gate to where the bank president, Homer Bradley, was seated at a large, well polished walnut desk, "Hello, Homer, lovely day wouldn't you say?"

"Mighty fine day, Mr. Murray. Is there something we can do for you?" Bradley stood and offered Pete a chair.

"Yes, I guess you can if you don't mind, I would like to get into my private safe for a minute." He sat down and pulled the saddlebags to his middle with both arms, undoubtedly, the banker could tell they were heavily packed.

"Why sure, I'll get the keys myself. Excuse me, I shall return momentarily."

Upon Bradley providing the key, Pete slipped into the private area, secure from the sight of onlookers. He unloaded the saddlebags and stuffed a goodly amount of cash into the pockets sewn inside the coat. Without losing a minute he then loosened his belt and placed the remaining stacks of currency around his waist, put the belt back in place and patted his newly acquired waistline. Once he felt secure with the hundred and fifty thousand dollars in place, he went back to Bradley's desk. He briefly made small talk and crushed the bags flat against his chest before saying good-by and sauntering to the front door.

He stepped from the bank, took in a breath, placed a hand on each side of the newly extended waist, and set his direction up the street toward the stairway leading to his loan office. Irish Pete inwardly congratulated himself on that bit of shrewd showmanship. If one of Claypool's men was watching, they'd have believed the money had been left in the bank. And if Claypool was to question Homer Bradley, the banker would testify to the money bags being emptied during Pete's visit.

The big Irishman walked the distance to *The Royal*, passed it by and went up the flight of stairs that lead to his office. After locking the door from inside, he pulled stacks of money from under his clothes and put it in a black leather valise. He then worked the combination to the little safe that sat under his desk, extracted the deed and claim papers he'd promised to deliver to Claypool. He set them on his desk.

Planning a speedy exit after handing over the deed, he determined not to use the safe as a hiding place for the money. He set the leather case behind a full floor-length curtain and adjusted the curtain to be sure it wouldn't disclose its wealthy visitor. Satisfied with the procedures, he pushed the moveable bookcase aside and slipped through it and into the closet in Rink Slater's office. Rink was there.

"What the hell are you doing?" Rink barked in his usual guarded, friendly manner when he was caught off guard by Pete's sudden appearance.

"I need your help, Rink."

The saloon owner defused, "You know you can count on me...what have you got yourself into this time, you rusty looking scally-wag?"

"You really don't want to know, partner. I'll only tell you, it's big!"

"Sounds interesting!" Rink studied Pete's face as the bawdy redhead removed his hat and wiped sweat from the lining and likewise his forehead under the locks of hair, "Big enough to get you killed?" Rink queried. He could tell that his friend might be in over his head.

"Big. That's all, Rink, just big." Pete tapped at his pockets, "I need a cigar."

"Here," Rink held an open box toward Pete, "you might take an extra. It looks to me like you're going to need it... and some whiskey too."

"No time for that right now...but I do need your help on something else."

"Like I said, anything at all."

"I need to have you go downstairs and *quietly* get my cousin, Kendrick...bring him up here, and please do it as not to garner attention."

When the saloon owner left the room Pete gave the whiskey another thought; he popped the cork and drank from the bottle. *Just enough to settle my nerves'*, he thought.

Four to five minutes passed. Pete puffed on the cigar, his mind engrossed on the events of the morning. Again he tipped the bottle and took two long pulls as he pictured how he would piece together the handing over of the mine claim and deed to Claypool, come tomorrow. The bulky Irishman knew he couldn't let his guard down, he was sure that Carlton Claypool hadn't become so wealthy by being a fool.

The office door swung open and banged against the wall. Pete reacted like a man climbing out the window of a brothel with his clothes in his hands and finding his wife standing there waiting for him. Once he caught full sight of Slats and Rick, he melted and regained his wits. "Boys, do come through them doors a little quieter, if you will…I thought somebody had done taken a shot at me."

Rink broke into a belly-laugh, his entire body jiggled. He pointed at the red-headed Irishman and shouted, "Big, huh!" He roared again, "Maybe too big!"

Pete raised the bottle to his lips and watched his friends shake with laughter, making him the brunt of their amusement. Pete then joined in; he could just imagine the image he displayed as they entered the room.

Through gulps of remaining giggles, Slats said, "Cousin, the last time I saw you look that-a-way was when I blew up the outhouse with you sittin' in it." The three of them let out a new chorus of laughter.

The bottle of rye whiskey didn't last long. Time had come for the conversation to turn to business matters at hand and Rink could tell that his presence somewhere else would serve the two card-shark cousins better…even though it was his office. Rink somehow felt comfort in being left out of the *big* event Irish Pete was sharing with his cousin, Slats. The look on the faces of the two showed the kind of deception that deeply defined Pete's previous remark when he told Rink that he *really didn't want to know.* "Hope you two don't get yourselves dropped down a well filled with snakes with whatever shenanigans you've got going on…I'll just leave you to do your conniving. I've got a couple of new girls downstairs that need tendin' to."

"Come on Slats," Pete motioned toward the secret passageway, "I've got something to show you." The huge smile on Pete's face was enough evidence for the skinny cousin – he could tell the meeting Pete had with Claypool at the mine had gone as they'd planned.

When the jovial examination of the stacks of money subsided, the cousins made plans for their exchange with Claypool the following day and laid out their scheme for leaving town.

Pete thought this was as good a time as any – it had waited too long already, "Now, cousin, tell me about the boy that hangs around…that Jimmy character…he ain't in this ya know, and you'd best get rid of him, and today or tomorrow ain't really soon enough. So tell me, Kendrick, what's with him…and what's it gonna be?"

Slats drew his hands to his chest, grasped the lapels of his tailored coat and gave a chest-swelling start, "He's been kinda like a partner," Slats hitched his voice along with lifting a cheek clear to an eye-winking, "a junior partner ya might say."

"A what?" Pete took on a sour scowl and frowned it away, "A what did you say? He ain't your kid is he?" Irish Pete's mouth gapped when he asked.

"Hell no!" Slats scratch at his temple, "Well, now…he came along with me when I was tending to some business a couple of times. It ain't nothin' I can't be shut of in a day or two."

Pete's mouth wrinkled, "I'm taking you at your word, Kendrick. This is too big and too late in the game to fold, cousin," he squashed his lips together, shook his head repeatedly and said, "don't let that kid get in the way…it could be the death rattle for both of us, I think you know that."

"Yea, I know it could…but it ain't. I'm fixin the problem – I swear."

CHAPTER NINETEEN - JIMMY DOSS, OUTLAW

The three lawmen were within five miles of reaching Globe. Hank had an old feeling from his outlaw-trailing-days come set in his gut. He was sure the two men he planned to kill would be there in the mining town. There was never a time that the feeling failed him back then and he was as confident this time as he'd ever been – he knew he was right.

Since leaving the Worsham place back in the valley Hank continued to be uneasy about Matt and Scoot. He wasn't sure how he'd deal with them when the time came that was to face and kill the men that shot his brother, Josh. Hank reined his horse to a stop under a huge sycamore tree, shifted in the saddle and then walked his mount to a small grove of willows that bordered the crooked arm of a shallow creek. He scanned the setting before he spoke, "Let's camp here for the night – not much daylight left and I'd like some time to get familiar with this Colt again," he fingered the grip of the .45 hanging from his gun belt, "and this looks like a good spot."

Matt Ragle and Scoot said nothing. They looked at Hank and then at each other.

The ex-Ranger figured their thoughts, "Naw, I'm fine, just wanted to make sure my hand knows where my gun is when it needs to." He loosened the cinch strap with a strong steady hand, "And I'd rather reach Globe in the morning sun - better than the edge of night."

Scoot Wilkens shrugged, "Sounds good to me, I was wanting some coffee anyhow."

Before sundown Sheriff Ragle and Deputy Wilkens witnessed the grooming of a Colt pistol fast draw that was like lightning! Not only was Hank quick to clear leather, but two times of the four he tried, he put six holes in a log that were spaced closer than the diameter of a coffee pot – and he did it at a distance of twenty yards. The two men with him would affirm that Hank Darcy was still the vibrant, resolute lawman that he was before the head wound he suffered two weeks ago.

Hank was up at first light. Coffee was started and breakfast fixins laid out before the others sat up and rubbed the sleep from their eyes. "Nice day." He added some dry

JIMMY DOSS · OUTLAW

sticks to the fire, "I wonder what's going on back in Silver City?" He slyly slanted his eyes in the direction of others.

Neither man attempted a response. Without turning his attention from the fire, Hank droned another remissive comment, "I hope March Halstead doesn't have the citizens all riled up and ready to shoot the first stranger that rides into town." Hank half turned to look at Matt from the corner of his eye.

"Ah, he knows better than to do that." Matt rubbed his chin. The expression on his face was uneven, and grew more so when he turned his eyes toward Scoot.

Matt's first glance at his deputy was questionable…he quickly turned his eyes to the campfire…but his mind was set on Silver City.

Hank started again, "Do you suppose Wallace Higgins recovered enough that he could give a good account of the robbers; maybe enough we could muster up more information," he hesitated and stirred a couple of maverick sticks back into the red glow under the flames, "that is, in the event they rode on past Globe and we need to circulate a dodger on them."

Everything was quiet for a spell. Neither Matt nor Scoot added any talk to the underpinning the ex-Ranger so casually manufactured. Following a brief meal of hardtack, bacon and canned peaches sent with them by Isaiah they broke camp and saddled up.

161

With his forefinger, Irish Pete tapped his cigar over the ash tin that sat on the front corner of his desk. It was filled, running over, with gray circles of ashes along with shredded bits of dark chewed peelings of tobacco leaves. The quiet in his office wore on his nerves. The evening seemed endless.

Next door and downstairs at *The Royal,* Slats McClary's attention was divided. His usual babble of cutting remarks was void at the table of high-rolling, suit-wearing men with diamond tie stick pins and gold watch chains dangling across their chests. He found the piano music especially irritating. He nodded a look over at the creator of the nonsensical noise every time his eyes rose to view his problem-partner, Jimmy Doss, standing on the other side of the room.

Slats knew this would be one of his last nights in Globe. The slick shenanigans he and Cousin Pete pulled on Claypool with the ten thousand dollars would be figured out by the rich mine owner once the reality set in that he'd spent a sizeable fortune on a silver mine that was worth about the same amount of money it would take to sit in for one evening of poker at *The Royal Saloon.* Perhaps it would take Carlton Claypool a week, or maybe two, after his discovery to link Slats and Irish Pete together, but he would surely put the pieces together once his investigation got up a good head of steam.

"You callin' that bet, Kendrick?" Al Hollings asked as he twisted his moustache, leaned and placed an elbow on the table between himself and Slats. "Or are you thinking you might want to get up and dance, the way you keep looking at the music machine over there?"

Everyone at the table laughed. The tall, lanky card-shark, who usually got the goat of others at the poker table, was the brunt of another man's handy work. Slats crossed a smile with a smirk and shook his head in appreciation of the snide remark. "I was just thinking that piano jockey needed a new pair of spectacles – he sure as bygone can't read the music with the ones he wearing." Everyone laughed again.

Jimmy Doss had stood quietly for a longer period of time than was usual. He made an impatient note of the interlude at the poker table, lifted his new watch from his pocket as he brushed the toes of his boots on the back of his trouser legs and casually started toward the door. Lillian would be waiting.

Slats gathered up chips and bills, tucked them all into a pocket of the brown tweed coat from Bong–Lo's, rose his tall frame and drawled, "Pardon me, gentlemen, I just recalled that I have a meeting with an investor friend in about ten minutes. I'll have to submit my chair to another donor." Amid the guffaws from his fellow poker players, he turned on his heel and made long strides to the door. As he exited the batwing doors, he saw Jimmy walking briskly toward the *Gem Saloon and Dance Hall.* Jimmy didn't know it but he was leaving town tonight. Slats earlier visit with Miss Russell had determined that. Now he watched the prelude to their plan begin to take shape.

Linda Russell knew of the love affair between Jimmy and her Lillian and felt it to be genuine. She'd regretfully told Slats that Lilly wasn't the kind of girl that generally rounded out her stable. She was too 'lady-like', not enough moxie. She'd accept the thousand dollars Slats paid her and see to it that the couple would be 'ushered out of town' unharmed. Miss Russell would mix the drinks herself and make sure the other money Slats left for the boy would be in his tote. By the time the meeting between the two had finalized their plan to deal with the young lovers each had quietly analyzed the checkered past that was a part of both of their lives. Perhaps time had begun to alter their contentious ways; a kindly consideration for someone else could be made. Of course the money helped to grease the decision!

As far as Slats could remember this was the only time in his life that he felt a soft spot for anyone since he went the outlaw route when he was eighteen. He thought about that notion all the way back down Main Street where the satirical feminine bursts of laughter were hushed by saloon walls and overridden by rinky-tink piano music. The hour was nearing midnight but the town was still very much alive. Typical loud mouth rowdies scuffled through the smoke infested parlors and a few stumbled along the boardwalks, making their way to yet another saloon. So long as they had some coins to clink together in a pocket they'd continue to try to drink their way to happiness. Tomorrow they'd make their way back into the tunnels, earn a dollar or two and they'd be eager to spend it all once again when the sun went down and the painted ladies bumped their soft, ruffled bodies from man to man in the drinking establishments of Globe.

The next morning, about the time the saloon workers were rearranging chairs and swatting drunks from the boardwalks, Carlton Claypool sent one of his henchmen to Irish Pete's loan office. He carried a message for Pete to meet Claypool at the bank, in the office of Homer Bradley at one o'clock – and bring the papers on the mine. Pete read the note, handed the man a dime, and told him to relate back to Mr. Claypool that he would comply with the requests in full.

He hustled the man out of his second floor office. Now Pete had to get a message to his partner, Cousin Slats.

The big Irishman swung the bookcase back and ducked his bulky frame into the passageway that led into Rink Slater's office. Thin slits of light outlined the secret doorway which separated him from the room at the opposite end of the small access way.

"Well, look what the cat drug in," Rink quipped. He twisted about in the handsome leather-tufted chair, "I hope you got an extra cigar in your pocket...you owe me, ya know."

"That I do indeed, friend. You surely know by now that I carry extras – just for you." The statement was as inaccurate as a blind man in a shooting gallery, but it'd served many times in the friendship between the two.

Rink knew the big nosed fella sometimes used the word *friend* when he was about to ask a favor. He laid back in his chair and waited as Pete raised from the shoulder height he'd assumed through the tunnel-like connection of the two offices.

The Irishman aligned his collar and pulled at the front of his coat, "I'll just trade you a ten cent cigar for a favor I need to ask of you, friend." He drew a cigar from a loaded vest pocket and handed it to Rink. "Have you seen that no-account-cousin of mine in your fine business establishment this morning?" Another compliment from Irish Pete, often accompanied by the request of a favor...Pete helped himself to a side chair.

"Haven't seen him," Rink remarked, and looked at Pete who had anxiety oozing from his face. He could see that his neighbor was loaded with anticipation. "Thanks for the cigar," the saloon owner said as he bit the off the tip and struck a match, "but if you want, I'll have one of my people search him out. He must be close by…this town ain't so big that my go-boy couldn't find him this time of day in an hour or so…if he had a little motivation – say a dollar or two." Rink widened his eyes.

Pete scooted the chair to the edge of the desk, took a pencil and paper and bent to write a note. Rink leaned back, cuddled the cigar between his thumb and forefinger onto his lips, drew in, and blew three quick rings of smoke over his head, waiting for Pete to compose the note.

When Irish Pete finished writing, he folded the paper, snatched up an envelope and wrote *'Kendrick McClary'* on it, licked the flap and sealed it against the desk with the palm of his hand.

"Okay, here's the message," he dug a finger into a breast pocket and extracted a pair of silver dollars, "and here's the motivation; where's your go-boy?"

CHAPTER TWENTY –
JIMMY DOSS, OUTLAW

After breakfast Slats went to the saloon where Jimmy and Lilly spent time together. He ordered coffee and settled at the end of the bar. Linda Russell, the owner, stepped from the door that led to her quarters, looked his way and stood with a raised hand placed on a column in the center of the dance floor. The second time she looked in his direction she nodded three times and flicked a wink. Words weren't necessary. She then began her normal morning sashay to the back of the bar. Slats knew the travel plans for the young couple had been carried out last night.

"So there you are, Mr. McClary." A beseeching voice caught Slats by surprise. He turned quickly and coffee lapped over the cup rim and onto his gray and blue plaid coat sleeve. He looked defiantly at the man that called his name and was walking toward him; an envelope extended from the man's outstretched hand.

Slats brushed the coffee from his sleeve and continued to glare at the fellow who had confronted him. Intentionally making the man wait, Slats pulled the hanky from his breast pocket, flipped the wrinkles out of it and swabbed at the coat. After inspecting his handiwork, he returned the white cotton cloth to the pocket before accepting the envelope.

He finished reading and looked up. The man remained steadfast in the spot he'd assumed with delivery of the message. Slats grimaced, cleared his throat and extracted a quarter from his pocket; giving it a second thought, he then selected a silver dollar and flipped it in the air for the man to snatch. "Any return message?" The go-boy asked.

"Nope, your job is done. I'll take care of it."

Slats knew better than to go directly to Irish Pete's office. Within minutes bright sunlight outlined his frame as he entered *The Royal Saloon*. He assumed a nonchalant manner and sauntered over to the bar and waved an index finger to the barkeep. When the heavily bearded man had closed the distance, Slats posed a question, "Is Mr. Slater in his office?" Having said that, the well dressed bank robber bent slightly and looked up the stairway.

"I'm sure he is, Mr. McClary. In fact he'd let me know, not more than an hour ago, if you came in I was to send you up."

- -

Hank set the saddle in place and reached for the cinch as he spoke to Matt and Scoot, "I want the two of you to pay a visit to the local marshal first thing when we get to Globe."

"You're not going in with us?" Matt questioned the ex-Ranger.

"No, I don't want the people in town to know who I am or why I'm there…it's different for the two of you, being lawmen from another territory, you need co-operation and support from the local law." Hank stuck a toe in the stirrup and swung up, "You two go on ahead, I'll be a few minutes behind so's nobody puts us together."

Matt Ragle and his deputy readily located the law office of Marshal Karl Houghton. And following simple introductions, Matt laid out the story of the bank robbery and killing of the bankers and Josh Darcy back in Silver City. "The folks in my town appreciate anything you can do to give us a hand – the loss of the money hurt a lot of them, but what's more, they want those men brought to justice for the killings." Matt gave descriptions of the outlaws as best he could, knowing one of the men was young, not much more than in his teen years, and the other one being unusually tall and thin.

Marshal Houghton sat at his desk, slump shouldered and hands folded on the desk top. He listened openly, but seeming unconcerned with details; very indifferent from the reaction Matt anticipated. The middle-aged, rumpled, Globe law man lifted his hat and ran his fingers through thin, immature graying hair, raised his chin to the ceiling, evidently in consideration of the descriptions, but he said nothing.

The two Silver City lawmen looked at one another, their expressions holding questions about Marshal Houghton's response. Matt leaned forward and placed his hands on the disorderly desk, "Have you seen anybody new in town that fits the description of either of the men?"

The Globe marshal shifted his eyes to Matt, shook his head and answered, "Nope...but then we get a lot of drifters with big ideas, thinkin' they's gonna come here and get rich...a lot of 'em. We know some are likely on the dodge from the law but we don't investigate ever man that shows up around here." Houghton fidgeted and wiped a hand across his mouth, "If I kept book on ever man what sets foot in Globe, I'd get nothin' else done."

Once again, the Silver City lawmen exchanged disparaging looks. Their expressions left no doubt – they were wasting their time with this man. Matt stared at the listless lawman and thought, *'The man just sits at his desk, maybe reading dodgers, and if he sees a familiar face on one, I'd bet he remembers to be sure and stay away from the culprit.'*

"Well, we're gonna have a look around town and see if we can turn anything up." Sheriff Ragle looked over at Scoot and nodded toward the door. "Thanks for your time."

"You'll let me know if I can be of help I suppose?" The second rate lawman muffled, "you can regularly catch me here...or if not here, up to the café across the street next to the hotel."

Once outside on the boardwalk, Matt shook his head, revealing his disgust, "I'm glad Hank wasn't with us, he'd probably have ripped that ol' geezer's head clean off. He's a shining example of what a lawman ain't suppose to be."

"I doubt that he'll wear that badge for long," Scoot said back, "some sensible, self respecting man will come along and put him outta that chair some day soon."

A shrill-voiced shriek sounding like a quitting time whistle from one of the mines filled the air, coming from a youthful, red-headed saloon girl running across the street a couple doors down from where Matt and Scoot stood. She was draped in a tangle of multicolored beaded necklaces that flew all about her painted face as she ran, dodging the ruts. She hefted her ruffled purple dress in one hand and had a fist full of paper money in the other as she shrieked and stumbled.

A rugged man with a full face of whiskers, dressed in filthy mining garb, lurched and floundered some thirty feet behind her. He shouted, "Give me back my money, you filthy no account…" He stopped and yanked a pistol from the hip-high holster at his side.

BOOOMMM!

The gun shot resounded like a stick of dynamite; the buildings holding the sound the same as a narrow canyon. The bellowing explosion left a ringing in a man's ears and the few people anywhere close by snapped their heads around and made for cover.

Matt pulled his revolver…, "Hey, YOU, STOP!" He leveled the gun at the grubby man.

The bushy-faced fellow stopped alright…and pointed the pistol at Matt. Matt jerked into a stance behind a splintery façade post as the deranged shooter unwittingly squeezed off two more BOOOMMS. The first slug struck a large glass pane fronting the apothecary store behind the lawmen, but the second caught Scoot in the arm just below the elbow. He grunted as his body twisted at the impact.

The street shooter clumsily started toward the lawmen, cursing and ready to continue his rampage. He held the six-gun shoulder high and stomped toward them in a frenzy.

Matt quirked a fleeting glance at his deputy – a flash of anger prodded him. '*Stay calm*'…Hank had instilled in him; '*make your first shot count*'. The young sheriff braced his revolver with both hands…his trigger finger squeezed smoothly – the Colt lurched and spouted flame.

The grungy man's head jerked forward, his body stretched tall and his toes drug backward as he twisted, one hand clutching at a spout of blood from his chest. He heaved and was down from Matt's slug.

The screaming woman disappeared into the *Eminence Saloon*.

An umbrella of quiet lapsed and heads poked out over swinging doors as wrinkled-brow onlookers timidly moved from storefronts to the street. The shooting wasn't an entirely unusual happening for Globe, with the exception of a woman being the target of a would-be killer.

Marshal Houghton peeked around the corner of his office door and reluctantly stepped into the sunlight. He saw Scoot Wilkins holding his arm at his side; blood flowed down the fingers of his hand and splotched the hardboards. The marshal moved forward and took note of the crowd that had gathered near the rumpled dead man lying in the street.

"It's over, marshal," Matt pushed the Colt into leather and lifted the palms of both hands toward the disinclined marshal.

"What the hell! You fellas shoot that man?" Marshal Houghton stood his distance from the two lawmen that'd just left his office.

"That man," Matt pointed a reluctant finger at the man sprawled in the street, "shot first. He shot at us – twice…hit my deputy." Matt levered a thumb toward Scoot, "My shot was in self defense. That man out there," he nodded and cut his eyes back to the street, "was chasing a woman. He pulled his gun and shot at her."

"She get shot too?"

"No, he missed…she ran into one of the buildings up the street."

"It's so's a man can't get through a day without somebody gettin' shot around here," the marshal grumbled. "You two come on back in my office, I'll send for the doc." He stretched his neck to view the man Matt had shot.

A bald headed gentleman in a shop-keeper's apron, his hands on his knees, was bent over the body of the dead man. The shop-keeper straightened and shouted at the marshal, "He's dead, Karl."

"You know him, Amos?"

The man wiped his hands on the apron and shouted back, "Nope, can't say as I do."

Under his breath, the marshal mumbled, "Likely another drifter the town's gotta bury." He pushed the door open and guided Scoot inside, "I figured you two for trouble when you showed…just didn't think it would come so soon. Sit there."

The slipshod but irritated Globe marshal shuffled more quickly than Matt had figured he could. He hurriedly shuffled his way back to the front door of the office, leaned out and yelled, "Amos, go get Doc Jacobs, send him in here." He hesitated, minced his lips, and shouted out the door again, "And Amos, while you're up to that end of town, send the undertaker down here after that man." He indicated the dead man with a flip of his head.

Hank Darcy had just ridden into town. From a distance, he witnessed the incident from where he sat his horse. He didn't want to disclose his identity or acknowledge his friends unless necessarily, but he wanted to know if Scoot had been hurt bad. He waited.

The doctor was in the law office less than a quarter hour. He and the marshal exited the building together. They were engaged in low key conversation when Hank came upon them, "Say, marshal, I don't mean to butt into your business, but I saw the shooting…I guess I need to clarify that…I saw all of the shootings – both men. The one that shot first at the woman who went into that dance hall," he pointed, "and then the man there in your office, when he returned fire at the man who was killed."

"So? What do ya want…a reward of some kind?" The marshal barked.

Hank was taken back a bit, "Well, no," he said, tucking his thumbs under his gun belt, "I figured if you needed a witness I could oblige you, that's all."

"Don't need no witness – them fellers there in my office are lawmen." The marshal drew his words out and pitched his head up and down, emphasizing the statement, "They was doing law work, and they told me what happened, that's all I need."

"Was that lawman that took a slug hurt bad?" Hank asked.

The doc responded before Marshal Houghton could put an answer together. "Got winged, that's all, no bones broke. At his age he'll heal in a week or so."

Hank tipped his hat to the men and quickly stepped off in the direction of the hotel where he planned to get a room. He'd find Matt and Scoot later, in his own time, when they were well distanced from the eye of the Globe marshal. *'Some lawman that old rascal is',* Hank said to himself under his breath as he lifted his watch from his vest pocket and continued his trek toward the hotel.

CHAPTER TWENTY-ONE –
JIMMY DOSS, OUTLAW

"This is it, cousin," Irish Pete smiled. He clapped his hands and rubbed the palms together like a pastry chef thinning dough. "This is the one, Kendrick...the one that I been waiting for." His voice was as merry as new bride standing before the preacher, smiling at her millionaire-about-to-be-husband, saying, *"Oh, yes I do!"*

Pete went on, "Like we figured Kendr...Slats, you're along to collect your twenty thousand." The giddy Irishman continued to fondle the thoughts of collecting another hundred thousand from Carlton Claypool.

All at once Pete's demeanor changed, the broad happy face was replaced by a tranquil but serious expression. He snatched the lapel of his coat, pulled it back and exposed the Pocket Colt .41, "I'm keeping this handy just in case it's needed."

Slats tapped at his side, "And I got one of my .44's like always," his demeanor was a reflection of that of his stocky, red-headed cousin.

The two men left the second floor loan office at ten minutes before one o'clock, the prescribed meeting time Claypool's message impelled. They walked toward the bank the next block over. Passing the gunsmith's shop at the corner, Slats took note of a man with deep blue eyes and black hair that appeared to measure him from head to foot, more than once. But he readily warded off the instinct that the man possibly held some sort of grudge against him, *'maybe a poker adversary from some time back',* he surmised, and turned his attention back to Irish Pete.

Hank Darcy dug into his pocket, pulled his watch and flipped it open. Time had passed quickly. He'd looked the town over for the past three hours and gauged numerous people. He'd also placidly inquired at business establishments, mostly saloons. He'd seen one man, a very tall man, who'd garnered his attention. But the man was much better dressed than the outlaw he pursued, and he was in the company of a gentleman that appeared to be a businessman, not the young person of the type that had been described to him.

Matt Ragle and Scoot walked their horses, heading for the livery at the east end of town. Hank knew the two of them would tend to their horses before the afternoon was to give way to the long shadows preceding sunset. Finding them would be easy.

In a matter of minutes he came upon Matt and Scoot. "Hello, gentlemen," Hank fingered his hat brim, saluting the lawmen in an inconspicuous manner that anyone who noticed would believe them to be strangers, "I wonder if you fellas might give a new man in town directions to the livery," Hank extended the role as he appeared questionable.

They read his mannerisms and both responded with a nod. Matt's reply was simple and easy. He rolled his head to the east, "We're heading that way ourselves, if you'd like to tag along."

"Don't mind if I do," Hank again flicked a finger and thumb to the hat brim and making sure to take notice of the sling on Scoot's arm, he carried on the charade, "How'd you hurt that arm mister?"

The three of them gathered at the corral, cautious not to tip their hand should someone give notice. Hank discreetly informed them that he'd witnessed the shooting and told them of his brief conversation with the marshal and the doctor.

"I've been thinking more about Marsh Halstead back in Silver City," Darcy thinned his lips and focused on Matt, "and I've not reconciled my feelings about what might be going on back there." Without more than a blink after saying that, he continued, "We've been gone for twelve days with the time I was laid up back at the Worsham place. The folks back home are surely getting more than a little fretful about us."

Matt's expression acknowledged the obscurity of Hank's words before he spoke, "I've been thinking about that too – don't want my town getting' turned upside down – me not being there." He turned his shoulders a quarter turn toward town, "That good-for-nothin' lawman we talked with wouldn't hardly give us the time of day. He didn't have a speck of interest in helping us to find them men we're chasing after. I don't believe he'd have told us even if he knew of them." Matt was perplexed, he pushed back his hat and tucked his fingers into the pockets of his jeans, "I figure he's as useless to this town as a pig that flies."

"I've been askin' around," Hank said, "and nobody seems to recall seeing anything of the outlaws. But I don't believe anyone would have said so if they did." He crossed his arms and looked toward town. "Maybe I'm wrong about the notion that they were headed for Globe." He looked over a shoulder, "They likely traveled on through here," he wrinkled his brow, "to who knows where." He didn't tell them about seeing the tall, well dressed man accompanied by the assertive red-headed business man with the big nose; a tall man he intended to learn more about later.

"I'm thinking it might be for the better if you two went home," Hank's remark was stern, yet lacked the fortitude he used when giving an order. "Scoot, that arm will be needing some attention and some time to heal, just another reason for you men to head on back." He studied Scoot Wilkens' eyes, "You wouldn't be much good in a fight if we had to make a stand, not if things got real rough."

The ex-Ranger was determined to move these two aside, to get them out of his way when he revenged the killing of his brother, Josh. If the long-legged skinny man he'd laid eyes on earlier was one of the killers, that time might come about sooner rather than later. Hank knew too that the local law would be of no help – but no hindrance either. Globe would be a good place for the stark, ranger-style justice he planned.

"What about you?" Matt remarked, "You ain't planning on dropping this are you?"

"Look at it this way, Matt, this is probably a lost cause; and if it ain't, who knows when or where it'll play out. I've been on the prowl for hard cases like those two many times, and mostly by myself." Hank's stance became more rigid, "I know how to handle myself and I've never put my neck through a hole that got it chopped off."

Sheriff Ragle looked down at the star on his chest; he gave it a little rub, "You helped put this badge on me, Hank Darcy, and I respect you for it. I guess I'll keep on respecting you and do as you ask." With that, he put a hand on his deputy's shoulder, "Scoot, we'll start back in the morning. Like Hank says, that arm of your will be needing some rest."

- -

The Irish cousins, Pete and Slats, arrived at the bank ahead of Claypool. One of the bank tellers saw them enter and walked the few steps through the railed outer office toward Homer Bradley's private office. The thump of his hard soled shoes stopped, "Mr. Bradley, they're here," he announced in a subtle tone.

Bradley looked up. He gave Pete and Slats a big smile through the wavy glass and signaled with a hand for them to join him. As they stepped through the door, he rose and extended his hand, "Hello, Mr. Murray." He turned toward Slats, "Mr. McClary, I believe it is," he looked up into Slats thin face, "I'm please to meet you. They shook hands and Slats dipped his head a couple of times in a manufactured show of appreciation.

"Good to see you again so soon, Mr. Murray." He swung his hand toward two of the four empty chairs that fronted his big walnut desk, "Have a seat gentlemen, I'm sure Carlt…er, Mr. Claypool will be here soon."

No sooner had the back sides of the men's pants hit the chairs until Claypool and two of his well-groomed, but tough looking associates, as he liked to refer to his bodyguards, stepped into the bank. A forth man holding a leather valise across his chest, dressed in a dark blue suit and wearing gold, wire-rimmed glasses sitting near the tip of his nose, followed closely. His black derby hat, when removed, exposed a wide bald path running from his brow to the back of his head. The Claypool group walked in military fashion toward Bradley's office.

"Oh my, I'll need to get another chair." Bradley rose, drew the attention of the bank employee who had earlier notified him of the presence of Pete and Slats, and with hand signals, ordered another chair brought into the private office.

Claypool stepped though the office door, "Hello, Bradley." His manner was blatantly confident yet void of conviction. He quickly turned his attention to Pete. "Mr. Murray," he removed his hat, and with a brackish nod at the red-cheeked man, he continued his 'hellos' with an extended hand in the direction of Slats, "Mr. McClary, I'm pleased that you could join us – and I want you to know that your good nature, and certainly," he drew the words out, "your astute sense of business…and I need to add," he hesitated in a moment of thought before he continued, "your capacity of masterfully assessing the resourcefulness of expedient

184

profit." The words rolled out of his mouth in the manner as that of a stage performer.

To the surprise of all in attendance, Claypool made a slight bow, drawing his hat slowly across the front of his body, "Perhaps you were aware," the performance continued, "of…shall we say, my absolute diligence in regard to securing possession of worldly matters that I desire."

Claypool's words would be assessed as either a brash statement, or a question, depending on the listener's interpretation.

Slats responded with a slightly knotted brow, a dip of his chin, and, "Yes, sir, my past has taught me to recognize that good fortune can be had if one will make proper judgment." He grinned inwardly.

"In the brief time I've known Mr. McClary here," Pete exuded a simple stage capacity of his own, "I've grown to admire his ability to size up a situation and respond most appropriately, especially at the poker table." Pete's rosy cheeks flexed as his head bobbed and a small laugh spilled out.

CHAPTER TWENTY-TWO – JIMMY DOSS, OUTLAW

The mixture of men gathered in Homer Bradley's office. Consummation of the mine sale was going to take place, however, parties of the sale and purchase had somewhat different perspectives as to just what was going to evolve over the next several minutes.

Claypool's armed *associates* stood with steely-eyed hard faces, one just outside of Bradley's door and the other stationed at the bank's front entrance, each with scatterguns draped over an arm and holstered revolvers tied down, hammer thongs off.

Small talk ceased and introductions finalized when Claypool lifted an arm toward the overdressed, stiff little man clinching the black leather case, "This is my lawyer, Mr. Fortney." Fortney's hands and arms appeared too occupied

186

with the valise to offer a hand shake. "He's drawn up the documents for this exchange and he also holds the money to be deposited in Mr. Bradley's bank."

That remark held the sustained interest of the Irish cousins as Claypool, with the wave of his hand, requested that the discerning man in the gold rimmed glasses step forward. He did so. And without hesitation he drew a key from a vest pocket, unlatched the valise and withdrew a series of papers that brought frowns from Pete and Cousin Slats.

With no further delay, Fortney upended the black case and emptied the contents onto the desk. "For your safe-keeping, Mr. Bradley, here is Mr. Claypool's one hundred and thirty thousand dollars," He drew his hands together at his waistline and laced his fingers, "I believe you can verify that we've accurately delivered the required sum?" The attorney's words directed the banker to the action of organizing the stacks of currency and setting them in rows appropriate for his count.

Bradley looked up and set his focus on Pete Murray, "One hundred and thirty thousand dollars – it's all here," his voice showed a sincere appreciation for the large amount of cash.

The hushed exuberance of the room was yet to settle before Claypool injected the next act, "I trust you have the claim papers and the deed, Mr. Murray?"

"Yes, I have them here in my pockets." He flashed open his coat, exposing a folded set of papers, one of which across the top, in bold letters, was the word 'DEED'. "But," Pete started, and couldn't get his words out quick enough…

"Wait a minute, Claypool, where's the twenty thousand I have coming?" Slats pulled his feet back from under Bradley's desk and lifted the frame of his long body in argument with the count of cash.

"That's all here in the agreement," Claypool's lawyer quickly interjected as he shifted one of the documents toward the side of the desk affronting the gangly man. "See right here," he pointed a well manicured finger to a paragraph on the second page, "that twenty thousand will be in the form of a certified note to be held by the bank with the cash we have here," his hand slid to hover over the cash that'd been neatly stacked by Homer Bradley.

Irish Pete cleared his throat. The grumble of dissatisfaction was clear.

The lawyer withdrew his hands from the paper he'd shoved in front of Slats and once again folded his fingers at his waist. He was fully aware that Irish Pete was awaiting explanation of the hundred and thirty thousand dollars that was, per the lawyer's description, '*to be held by Bradley – in his bank*'. "Yes, Mr. Murray, do you have a question?" Fortney widened his eyes, directed at the big Irishman.

Pete shifted in his chair and fronted his large body toward Claypool, "What in tarnation you tryin' to pull here...that money is leaving this bank today...with me... it's not staying here!" Pete knew his Irish temper had taken over. He took a deep breath. He realized he would think more clearly if the temper was drawn down. He continued, the gruffness softened, but the redness still glowed in his face, "I don't like what I'm hearing! You want to lease this mine, or buy it?" He wasn't looking for an answer; that was a limited confrontational way of expressing his displeasure, nothing more.

No sooner had the words crossed his lips than he remembered that the bank president, who sat across the desk, was of the opinion that he had stashed a sizeable amount of money in his private safe, leaving it at the bank. He needed some time to think. He looked up at Slats, who continued to stand, his lengthy fingers spread across the paper that Fortney had slid in front of him. Their eyes met; anger and frustration as visible as a bull at a tea party.

Pete turned toward the rich mine owner, his eyes narrowed, "Claypool, what you're doing here wouldn't be proper in a card game, and I don't consider it righteous in this deal either." He purposely fell short of calling him a cheat. "I'm going to listen to what your word-jockey has written, but this deal may have to back off. I just might

Don Russell

renegotiate with Mr. McClary here, since you seemed to reopen negotiation on your part."

Claypool lifted his chin and his nostrils flared, "I don't think you want to do that Mr. Murray." The harrowing sneer he threw at Pete almost brought a chill to the air. "You see, it's this way, Mr. Murray…if you don't sell that mine to me – and I consider my offer, and the conditions of my offer, quite upstanding and principled – I just don't believe you'll be able to sell it to anyone else." He brushed an invisible blemish from the sleeve of his very expensive suit coat. "In this town my money buys the best…or the worst, if you know what I mean…of anything!" Carlton Claypool cast his eyes to the heavily armed *associate* standing near the meeting room. He then extended both arms, his hands held palm down, "Let's all relax. You've not heard the content of the documents. I believe you will come to understand, and once you understand, you will agree that the terms and conditions, Mr. Murray, are reasonable and acceptable – if I may say so." With that, he lowered his chin to his chest and looked up under his brow at the men around the table. All grew quiet…still uneasy, but quiet. "Please Mr. Fortney, if you will."

Irish Pete realized Claypool held the trump cards. He pursed his lips, "No need to read the sale price; we all know that…and it ain't changin'…just get to the conditions."

190

Slats rubbed his chin, and holding back the impulse to pull the .44 from under his coat, he was somehow able to say calmly, "No need to read about the twenty thousand comin' to me, Mr. Lawyer. I've been hi-jinked by people like you before. Your words can be drippin' honey but end up saying that a man hates his ma." He thumped his fist on the desk, "I'll get my twenty thousand here and now!"

"Thirty days," Claypool shouted, "that's all, just thirty days," his voice dropped a full five octaves on the second 'thirty days'. "This is a lot of money. A reasonable man would understand," he asserted. "Let's take a minute…" he glared at the banker, "you got a bottle of whiskey handy, Bradley?"

Thirty minutes and a half bottle of sour mash later, the lawyer completed alterations to the documents, and within ten minutes more, signatures were etched in place and blotted dry by the bank president. Eighty thousand dollars was stacked to the side and handed over to Irish Pete Murray, twenty thousand of which was to pay Kendrick McClary. The balance, fifty thousand dollars, plus the certified note payable to Peter Murray would remain with the bank, that cash and note was to be controlled by Bradley, according to the escrow agreement.

Tempers were drawn back. Irish Pete had pushed with all of his reasonable persuasion for all for of the cash to be delivered to him now! He even had Bradley attest that he'd left money in the bank earlier; a point that wasn't true, but Bradley's comprehension of Irish Pete's prior bank visit seemed to verify his claim.

Claypool wouldn't budge any further. Fifty thousand had to remain in the bank.

Slats fumed inside but he knew that further argument from him might tilt Claypool's thinking. And either he, or his lawyer, Fortney, might catch on!

'Two hundred and thirty thousand dollars is a lot of money to gamble away', Irish Pete kept telling himself. *'We've got that much…I don't like leaving fifty thousand behind…but!'*

The meeting was over. The deed to the mine was signed over by Irish Pete. Claypool and Fortney gathered up the fifty thousand dollars, and along with the certified note, placed it back in the valise. Fortney handed it to Bradley, "For your safe keeping in your vault, Mr. Bradley."

Carlton Claypool felt he'd done a good job of protecting his interest. The original one hundred and fifty thousand he'd paid Pete Murray was in Bradley's bank, so he thought, and if Irish Pete attempted to take it out of the bank, Bradley would get word to Claypool before the Irishman could clear town. Another fifty thousand of his money was in escrow for thirty days. His only real concern, so far as he knew, was the eighty thousand that Irish Pete and McClary was walking out with today. Claypool figured the odds to be in his favor.

Claypool followed the Irish cousins to the bank's front door. He slapped Pete on the back like he was an old friend and barked a shadow of a laugh, "That mine had better be of the quality and nature represented, Murray." He then added, almost as an afterthought, "I don't suppose you'd have any idea of leaving town…of course not! You'll be a very rich man in a month and you can go anywhere you'd like, maybe even back to Ireland to visit and show your folks back there what a brilliant business man you are here in America."

"Like I said just a few minutes ago, Mr. Claypool, I ain't leaving, got no plan to…and that money of mine that's in the bank's holdin' better not leave either." Irish Pete shook a finger at Bradley, who stood behind the lot of them. "For now, this money is going into my desk lock-up back at my loan office. I'll be back, Mr. Bradley, for the cash I left with you before," he lifted his head indignantly, "and my fifty thousand cash…and the twenty for that note, in thirty days."

Slats stepped onto the boardwalk in front of the bank, lifted a cigar from his breast pocket and pointed it at Carlton Claypool, "You're a hard man to best, Claypool. I would have liked to have that mine. It's a better outfit than the one I had down in Tombstone, but I was a poker player before I ever was a mine owner. I like the easy money gathered from table tops better than diggin' for it in them dirty holes in the ground.

They all went their separate ways, each feeling the satisfaction of having bested the other.

CHAPTER TWENTY-THREE – JIMMY DOSS, OUTLAW

Irish Pete and his secretive cousin, Kendrick Slats McClary, together stepped into the bright sun that blanketed the front of the building. They seemed to share a discouraged expression; but if a man stood in the right spot on the broad, bleached boards, he could see a small wink, pass between them. They stepped down from the boards onto the street and stood in close conversation. The frowns they cleverly wore in deception were opposite to the words spoken as they placidly congratulated themselves, agreeing that it wasn't the results they'd desired, but it was *'one-hell-of-a-nice-haul'*.

They walked several steps together in the street. When well beyond Claypool or anyone else that might be watching, Pete placed a hand on Slats' arm, they halted and Pete spoke quietly, "We'd best separate." He casually surveyed the surroundings, and said, "Claypool's not going to let us out of his sight. His men will watch any move we make for at least a couple of days to see if we show any sign of travel."

"No doubt." Slats tapped ashes from his cigar, "I figure in three or four days Claypool's men will lighten up…and when they do," he briefly looked away from Pete and then finished, "we'll have our chance to vamoose this town."

Pete searched the street and boardwalks with abbreviated glances. He leaned close again, "With this kind of stake we can get ever thing we need in San Francisco…," he smiled, "we might just buy us a legitimate business once we get there." They shared a subtle chuckle; neither of the two took that statement to have much probability.

Slats slapped Pete on the back, and speaking up now, said, "I'll see you tonight, Murray." He held the cigar to his mouth, tilted back his head and blew a large bloom of smoke into the high, blue sky, "We'll have us a dandy of a poker game."

Slats started off toward his hotel and Irish Pete stepped out in the opposite direction toward his loan office next door to *The Royal*.

— —

The following morning, just after sunrise, a light shower settled the dust around the livery. Matt Ragle and Scoot, his arm in a sling, saddled up. A thin layer of gray stretched above the horizon. The air smelled of dampness. That odor, together with the stables, hid the smell of fresh biscuits and frying bacon in the little adobe house alongside the livery. It belonged to the Hensleys, who managed the livery.

Elmer Hensley saw the men preparing to leave. "Put on some more of that hog-back momma, I know them young fellas ain't had time to get up town for breakfast. They's going clear on down to Silver City, and one of 'em with that broke arm. We'll give them some hot vittles before they start out."

Elmer pushed open the door and stepped out, "Hey… you two! Come on in here," he shouted as he waved a hand with a come-on.

Matt cupped a hand aside his mouth and answered back, "We left money in the barn there – it's on the rail just inside the door."

"Naw, not that," Elmer bellowed, "come in here and get some morning vittles before you take to the trail. We got hog-back, biscuits, and lots of strong, hot coffee. Come on in."

"Why not." Matt jawed to Scoot. The two early risers stepped down and laced the reins over the rain-slick top pole of the fence.

- -

Hank lingered in the café longer than usual. The coffee tempered the cool, damp mountain air and gave him some time to think. His thoughts were about home, his wife Kate, and the kids. But the image of his younger brother, Josh, lying in the wagon, dried blood caked to his face and in his hair, pushed to the front of his mind. And he thought about the moments when he placed Josh in the casket he and Matt constructed. Was it good enough?

He shook the images from his head. He had to concentrate on the matters at hand.

Hank pulled himself together. He mentally reassessed the places he'd scrutinized in Globe. He thought about Marshal Houghton, the barkeeps, owners of the drug store, the mercantile, and the gun shop where he questioned the owners about men who might have been in their shops that would fit the descriptions. And what about the very tall business man he'd observed…that man didn't appear to be the type he was searching for, but then the people who had offered details of the outlaws always emphasized the height of one of them. That man was the tallest man he'd seen in Globe and much taller than most any man Hank had ever laid eyes on.

There were a lot of young men in Globe; a lot of them could be the young-looking man he was searching for. How could he sort that out?

Come to think of it, he hadn't yet thought to try to put the two together. He hadn't asked questions about seeing a tall man *with* a young, blond headed man who spent time together.

That's what he'd do today. He'd concentrate on trying to find them that way, somehow to place the two, a tall man and a young blond man as a team. The thought brought anxiousness to the ex-Ranger. He quickly downed the rest of the coffee, took a pair of nickels from his pocket and slapped them to the table top.

Saloons. That's where they all go – some more than others, but they all visit saloons! There were at least twenty-five saloons in Globe. Surely there would be somebody working in one of them would remember seeing a very tall, skinny man with a yellow-haired, young man!

The morning had been void. Hank made his way in and out of seven saloons without any luck. He'd talked with barkeeps and saloon girls. Most of them started shaking their heads back and forth before he'd finished with descriptions. It was plain and simple, the *'don't know'* ailment that the town marshal was afflicted with was a Globe epidemic. Those that would hear him out, he figured, did so only because they were more courteous, but he'd encountered the same illness in towns all over when he was a Texas Ranger – people didn't want to become involved. For most it was fear that if they gave information that caused trouble for a thief or no-account, the person would find out and put their neck on the chopping block.

It was drawing on past noon when Hank wandered into the *Gem Saloon and Dance Hall*. He set his wrists on the bar's edge. The barkeep looked up from the suds-filled sink. Hank raised a hand and waved an index finger at the barrel lying on its' side behind the counter, "Beer, please."

The barkeep nodded and toweled his hands on the grimy white apron as he shuffled over. "That'll be a dime."

"Huumm…been paying five cents ever where else in town," Hank quipped back at the long faced man.

"Well, if you're a dancin' man you just bought yourself a turn with a lady along with the beer, but the beer's a dime either way." He placed his hands on his hips as he goggle-eyed Hank, "You must be new in town." He juggled his head up and down while measuring the ex-Ranger, "Seems I have to say them words at least nine…ten times a week. He shifted his eyes to the rear of the room where three young women sat. They were dressed in gaudy, ankle length skirts with bands of lace at the waist and bosom. Color adorned their faces and droopy ribbon bows made attempts to hold the long curls falling over their ears.

Hank said nothing. He took two swallows of beer and set the mug on the bar, turned and looked toward the back of the dingy room following the gaze of the barkeep. One of the curly-headed *ladies*, sporting a toothy grin and a bouncing bosom glided toward Hank with an empty glass in her hand. She settled in beside him like a chicken returning to roost. "Howdy, handsome, you like to be friendly with a lonely lady who's thirsty?"

'Just like the old days', the dark haired, blue-eyed man thought to himself, *'things don't change much in these places'.* He offered a thin, fictitious smile "Sorry, don't dance…but I'll buy you a drink." He motioned for the bartender, "Bring this lady," he looked at her glass, "another of whatever it is she's drinkin'."

The paltry barman reached under the counter top, lifted a caramel colored bottle, popped the cork and splashed the short glass half full of the bottle's contents, stepped back and placed the bogus bottle back under the bar where he'd gotten it, "That'll be two bits."

Before the painted-faced young woman could wrap her fingers around the drink, Hank placed his hand palm down on the glass, drew a silver dollar from his vest pocket and plunked it into the tawny liquid and again placed his palm atop the drink. "Tell you what, young lady," he forged a seemingly genuine smile and looked her in the eye, "I'm looking for my nephew; if you'll tell me if you've seen him, the dollar and the drink are yours." Hank Darcy cocked his head slightly and stared into her placid hazel eyes.

She jerked her chin down only an inch and slanted her eyes up to his, "Okay." She picked up the glass and nodded, held it under her chin momentarily, looked back up at Hank, and slowly poured the contents through her rosy lips. "So what's this nephew look like?" She asked with a half grin as she fingered the dollar from the glass.

"Well, his most notable feature would be his shaggy blond hair. He was with his uncle, a man about this tall," Hank raised his hand several inches above his own head, "and skinny as a rail." He waited a second or two for any response before he went on, "My nephew's name is Jimmy."

Her eyes lit up…but the expression quickly disintegrated as her gaze went beyond Hank with concern. "He was here…had a crush on one our ladies…came in every night, sometimes more than once, and also came by during the day on some occasions." The woman's features softened, along with her voice, and she cast her scrutiny past Darcy, "But neither him, nor her, have been around for a couple of days. The tall man was in a day or two ago, didn't stay long though. I see most of the people who come in cause I'm here every day from a little before noon till…whatever time it takes!"

CHAPTER TWENTY-FOUR – JIMMY DOSS, OUTLAW

Hank took a long look around the *Gem Saloon*, and then back at the dancehall girl with the painted face and carelessly curled hair. He thought about the killing of the mountain man's woman. Any man who would kill a woman who was alone in a mountain cabin would have to be smitten, a crazy man without morals or feelings. He'd be a man that was likely to be attracted to a place like this...to young women like what worked here.

"You say you haven't seen my nephew or the girl...where would they have gone?"

"How would I know, I ain't hardly been outta this place for more'n a year. Me and my friends over there," she flipped her head toward the other two dancer girls, "we just figured they run off. They was pretty stuck on one another – if you know what I mean."

Hank saw the girl's expression change. A sudden glow of fright came to her face and her mood grew as cold as a winter wind blowing through a crack.

"I got to go now mister," her eyes fluttered, but this time with dreaded anxiety. She quickly shuttled past the ex-lawman and headed for the back of the room.

Hank's focus aligned to the direction the girl last looked before she hastily retreated. A woman dressed in fashionable, over-ruffled, satin finery had entered the room from what was evidently an entrance door to private quarters. She was Linda Russell, the owner of the saloon and dancehall.

The woman sashayed toward Hank. Her smile was friendly but he could tell that she wanted to know what had gone on between him and the dance girl. She could tell from the girl's method of retreat that it was her presence that compelled the girl's anxious departure.

"Hello, stranger; I don't believe I've seen you in here before," Linda Russell cooed as she looked him up and down. "I saw you were talking with Helen." Her smile expanded, "If you'd like to get to know her better, I can arrange it."

"Well, no, I was asking her about my nephew, Jimmy."

The jolted look that Ms Russell responded with had more information wrapped in it than any words she could have spoken. Her face became rigid - but she dropped the tempestuous expression as quickly as a snuffed candle ceases to emit light. "Don't know as I know of anyone around here by the name of Jimmy." Her lips tightened and melted into a fabricated smile. She blinked and asked, "Did Helen know of a Jimmy?"

Hank could tell he'd gotten all the information he was going to get, and he knew the girl would have trouble if he told this woman what had been divulged. "She just said she thought she's heard another of the girls call a young man Jimmy, but she wasn't real sure."

"Is that all she said?"

"That's about it." Hank thumbed the brim of his hat, "Thanks, Miss, I'll guess I'll be getting on with my search; there's a lot of saloons in this town, maybe somebody's seen him, and if so maybe I can find him and take him back to his folks in Texas."

Hank pushed through the swinging doors and looked back over his shoulder. Ms Russell had a handful of her skirt in each hand and was on a fast, straight line toward her private door.

"If I was a prospector I'd say I found color, maybe the mother lode!" The ex-Ranger whispered to himself. He needed to think, to sort out the pieces of information he had. *That tall man…if he was the one I now think he just might be…why is he still in town? But not Jimmy? I wonder how that adds up?'* He needed coffee. When he was on the warm trail of a fugitive and had some things to ponder about how to snap the trap shut, looking into the cup of steaming coffee for a few minutes had always helped.

He went to the café down the street. As he put a boot toe on the step leading up to the door, he turned and, *'Yes he could see the front doors of The Gem Saloon'.* He took a seat by the front window and ordered coffee.

It was getting late in the day. Hank sat in a chair with a good view of the main street and watched the people of Globe come and go. He thought maybe he'd catch sight of the unusually tall man once again. Shoddy dressed miners with dusty clothes and mud caked to their boots were beginning to mingle with the regular townies. A good portion of the men who hefted ore also hefted vile language that was resented by the lady-folks of the town's men. Their men, through some unwritten law somewhere, were required to abide by that thinking as well.

In the past hour the number of women on the boardwalks had dwindled to near nothing and the street population had gotten heavy with miners and no-accounts, some gamblers, and an occasional drifter with easy-money on his mind.

Hank Darcy saw Marshal Houghton amble up to, and then inside, the *Eminence Saloon,* the saloon the woman ran into when she was chased by the culprit that shot at her; also the man that shot Scoot in the arm Matt Ragle had to kill the first day they arrived in Globe.

Darcy had been void of ideas the past couple of hours, *'I think I'll see what that two-bit lawman is up to…'* He ducked into the door of the *Eminence* and readily shifted to one side. The marshal stood at the bar appearing to question the barkeep. A minute later, the marshal set a glare to the back of the head of the bar man as the man walked away from him the full length of the counter top. There the bartender stood with folded arms and a twist of his neck as he glared back at the marshal. He'd given Marshal Houghton the information he wanted but disliked doing it. The marshal had used a name that could cause trouble.

"Can I buy you a beer, marshal?" Hank asked, having moved quickly, but silently, to the shoulder of the slouchy lawman.

Houghton turned on his heel. He squinted at Hank – a spark rose in his face, "You still in town?"

Hank just nodded.

"I don't drink." The marshal etched an answer to Hank's offer to buy.

"Don't drink – then what are you doing in this place?"

"Law business," Marshal Houghton's narrowed eyes scrubbed Hank from head to toe. He seemed to feel that he needed a broader barrier set between his blunt answer and the 'law business' comment. His mouth opened to form a word but nothing came out…he blinked and gave it another try, "I'm investigating that woman – the one that was bein' shot at." His eyes switched side to side under the wire-frame glasses. The ex-Ranger could tell that the work-shy ol' coot probably wasn't here of his own volition.

"I thought you'd let that incident rest?"

"Well," his hand went to his mouth and nose; he rubbed, as was a habit of men trying to gather their wits, "the man that was killed by that high-falutin' lawman from Silver City, well, he was an employee of a man named Claypool, a pretty important man here in town," he drew a deep breath through his nose, "and a friend of mine." Houghton flexed his shoulders and went on, "The money that woman stole from the crazy bastard who was chasing after her was actually Mr. Claypool's money. Me being' the law," the grizzly indolent slapped at the badge on his chest, "I'm gonna arrest her and get that money back to its' rightful owner." He snapped his lips together and manifested a challenging snarl to sling at Hank.

"Sounds like you're doing a fine job…one to be proud of," Hank's tone left little to sort out, but he figured the marshal couldn't see through it. The coincidental meeting with Houghton brought to his mind that his friends, Matt and Scoot were to have left town this morning.

The marshal didn't mention any intention of investigating them, but in-as-much as Houghton had an allegiance to some man named Claypool; and the tumultuous, whiskered man that Matt shot and killed was an employee of his, Hank thought it a good idea to see if they'd cleared out as planned. He started off toward the livery.

"Howdy there, Mr. Darcy, you wantin' that big black horse of yours?" Elmer Hensley asked as he stood with tack draped over this arm.

"Nope. I'll be staying in Globe another couple of days, I reckon." Hank stretched his neck, making a quick inspection of his own, "but I wondered if those two lawmen from Silver City have been around this morning?"

"Yea, but they readied up and rode out not long after day break," Elmer studied the sun's position in the sky momentarily, "about six or more hours ago, I'd say. You got business with them boys?"

"Naw, I'd seen the shooting they was in, where the one fella took a slug in the arm. I was of a thought to how he was getting along, that's all." Hank tipped his hat, "Much oblige, I'll be heading on back…there's a man I want to see up town." He half turned then turned back, "Oh, yea, there, hostler, you wouldn't happen to know a man named Claypool, would you?"

"Why everybody here in town knows Carlton Claypool, he's maybe the richest man around these parts. Nye-on to everyone," he looked around, cautiously searching out any set of ears that might hear, "kisses his…behind! Ya know what I mean?"

"Well, it seems that most any town has one of them kind…don't know why Globe would be any different." Hank Darcy broke a slight grin, "Thanks," he turned once again."

"My name's Hensley…Elmer Hensley, mister."

The ex-Ranger knew the man was fishing for his name, but Hank just shook his head up and down and waved over his shoulder in acknowledgement.

The livery sat more than a hundred yards apart from the business part of town. He walked beneath a big sycamore tree as a breeze rousted up a memory of the day they buried Josh on the grassy knoll beneath the big tree. Sadness gripped him. And then anger wrestled into his mind, the memory of Josh, the dried blood, Kate crying…it all fell on his shoulders once again. He stretched an arm down his side and fingered the Colt Peacemaker. Like old times, he couldn't allow the righteous side of him to outstrip his purpose – he was on a mission. His lips moved in a silent, autonomous manner as he again silently promised Josh that his death would be reconciled before he would again set foot on the Box-D soil of home.

In the shadowed distance Hank could see a man working his way along the street with a ladder in hand, lighting the oil lamps.

CHAPTER TWENTY-FIVE – JIMMY DOSS, OUTLAW

Slats was tired and more than a bit uneasy about not getting the other seventy thousand from Claypool. It had been a long, prosperous day for the Irish but there were problems that had to be worked through in order to hightail it out of Globe.

The dim light of dusk gave way to nightfall. For now the crafty, lean outlaw needed to rest a bit. He'd partake of a brief nap then wash up and make his way over to *The Royal* for poker as planned.

Slats made his way to the Emerald Hotel, up the single flight of steps and to the room he'd shared with Jimmy before having his young partner removed from Globe. He stopped. The door was ajar. Slats backed up a pace, pulled back his coat and slowly lifted the Russian .44 from leather.

He held it high to his chest with both hands, one on the barrel and the other clinched the grip, trigger finger in place. He turned his head sideway and cautiously peeked through the narrow opening. There was a woman staring into the top drawer of the dresser. One hand was in the drawer she'd opened and the other rested with her fingers on top, bracing her as she crooked her neck and looked.

The gangly Irishman placed the business end of his .44 against the hard wood adjacent to the numbers, and gently pushed the door inward. "Ooohh," she gasped and turned in reflex to the faint creaking sound. The large pendant earrings swung wildly against her cheek as she simultaneously shoved the drawer shut with a thud and blurted, "Oh-my-God!"

He recognized her immediately, "What is it you'd be looking for, Ms Russell?" Slats voice was melodiously redolent, couldn't have been sweeter under the circumstances.

Linda Russell smiled her best smile, contorting her pleasantly defined lips in a manner that suggested Slats was about to be kissed with a very romantic kiss. "Well of course, I was looking for you, Mr. McClary." Her deep blue eyes danced with passion.

"It don't take no over-sized brain to know I couldn't fit in that drawer," he scowled…, "so now tell me again…what are you looking for?"

She cupped her hands to her bosom, "Well, Mr. McClary, I really was looking for you…since you weren't here I…I…became concerned, and naughty little me…well I just thought I'd search a mite for some little something that might lead me to you." She very gracefully moved her head from side to side to accentuate her femininity.

Slats holstered his pistol and lowered his extensive frame into a ladder-back chair that he hedged in front to the door. "Okay, you found me! Now just tell me what is it that brought you…and don't put out a line of that crap your girls powder up them dunces with over at your dance-hall. I ain't in the mood for no nestin'."

She grew solemn. Her overt charm turned hard and dry as a piece of sliced bread that'd been left out all day. "I don't know where he is." She made the matter-of-fact remark and then stood with her hands propped on her hips.

"What the hell do you mean…where who is?"

"That boy… Jimmy, the one you had me shanghais last night…that's who." She stared at Slats like she was challenging him – like it was his fault – not hers. "The men I had take the two of them, Lilly and your Jimmy," Linda's hands flailed as she talked, "…they came in the hall just a few minutes ago and told me he'd give 'em the slip about sun up this morning. I came right over…Christ, I didn't know where you were," she hesitated and took a breath through clinched teeth, "but I knew you'd want to know." With that she dropped her backside onto the bed, thumped

213

her hands palms down on either of her hips and fixed her gaze on the floor.

Slat's mind shifted from a little pissed off to branding-iron hot. With a clinched fist, he erupted from the chair and took one of his long strides toward her.

She flinched a melodramatic retreat in the face of an arduous predicament. The life style she'd chosen wasn't one for a feeble, diffident coward, but she played it well.

They then exchanged loud, boisterous barbs, each giving the other what for; finally ending when each of them realized their dispute wasn't to be settled here and now.

"Damn!" The lean, underweight man stood in the center of the dim, indistinct room, his skeletal body fixed in place, the anger subsided and he peered at the dance-hall-madam as if she might have been a meal grown cold. "You owe me a thousand dollars, ya know!"

There was no response. Her made-up eyes didn't even blink as she congealed into a decorated, delicate statue. The two of them remained steadfast, eye to eye, like a pair of alley cats, each sizing up the other.

"Did the boy know I was in on it?"

"He had no idea. I'd instructed my men to tell the two love birds nothing. For all they knew, they was being thrown out because she was treating him to unpaid favors."

All grew quiet again.

Ms Russell was the first to move. She wiggled her high-heeled shoes, slowly drew her legs out from under the green silk dress, pushed against the bed and stood upright. "Yea, okay...I owe you a thousand!" Her voice was gruff and nearly masculine, "If my men find him, and they do the job right this time, I'm keepin' it." Linda Russell tucked and smoothed her dress, shifted her bosom with the heels of her hands and lightly touched her hair all around in preparation to depart. Prior to stepping through the door, she pushed against the drawer that she'd been meddling in, "Nothin' there worth while anyway," she offered in huffy rebuttal of the circumstance in which she'd been discovered.

Slats removed his new Stetson hat he'd bought just before returning to his hotel room...sort of a personal congratulatory reward to himself for the magnificent deception he and Pete had parlayed into a small fortune. He had his eye on it in the window of the mercantile for the past week. He tossed it to the center of the bed as the door slammed shut. Ms Russell's steps ka-plunked down the hallway and faded into oblivion.

The tall, and now rich, man kicked a valise from under the bed and set it on the chest of drawers. He put a fresh shirt and a pair of riding pants in the case, deciding he couldn't take more clothes. He laid a Smith & Wesson pocket gun he'd won in a poker hand on top of the twenty thousand dollars from Claypool and eight thousand dollars left from the Silver City Bank. He then placed the banded roll of six sticks of dynamite on top, shut and locked the latch.

The extra clothes Slats had obtained since being in Globe were left hanging in the chiffonier along with some new boots, string ties, socks and underwear. If any of Claypool's hounds did get into his room they wouldn't know but what he was still in town. And, if Jimmy came back to the room, he would see that his personal belongings were still there. That would help to convince the boy Slats had nothing to do with the disappearance.

Ex-Ranger, Hank Darcy leaned against the corner of the leather shop. He'd been in place not more than five minutes when he saw the large red-headed man who he'd seen with the tall gentleman two days ago.

Pete Murray walked out of the tobacco store a hundred feet or so from where Hank stood. The bulky-framed man made his way up the boards in Hank's direction and stopped in front of a saloon that Hank hadn't yet investigated, *The Royal*.

Irish Pete puffed on a large cigar as he stood talking with a pair of men dressed in finely tailored suits of clothes. *'Friendly chatter'*, Hank conceded, nothing more…just business men with nothing much to do.

Pete swiveled his head up and down the street several times as the conversation continued in what seemed to be a jovial subject to all three. He held the stogy in his mouth under the rust colored moustache and manufactured smoke like a miniature steam engine. Pete's hands gyrated with each word as he dominated the conversation, his head playing the same melody as his hands. Soon the group exchanged open-handed slaps to each other's shoulders and they all went their separate ways.

Hank paid attention to Pete in-as-much as he'd seen him before with the very tall man. He watched as Pete puffed and walked his way into an off-the-boards foyer; an overhead sign indicated it to be the entrance of IRISH PETE'S LOAN OFFICE.

Hank continued to hold up the corner of the building and observe for several more minutes.

Enough! The broad-shouldered ex-lawman crossed the street and selected a route that would take him to the stairs where he'd observed the cigar puffing Irishman.

Darcy ascended the steps and after turning to look back down the stairs, he wrapped his knuckles on the solid oak door. No Answer. He knocked again. Again, no answer. He tried the knob. Locked. He twisted the knob more assertively. Still no good. Hank removed his hat and placed an ear against the door. He heard nothing. *'That's strange – I know I saw that fella come up here – where else could he have gone'?*

CHAPTER TWENTY·SIX – JIMMY DOSS, OUTLAW

Irish Pete ducked through the passageway. He needed a drink.

"You in there, Rick"?

"Come on in."

"Would you offer me up a drink, ol' friend…seems I'm empty again."

"Help yourself, you know where it is."

"I don't have much time, but was needin' a little glow down my pipe."

"Take what ya' need." Rick looked back to his desk, "I've got to get this letter finished…so if you'll give me a couple minutes…"

Pete took a drink and held the bottle out in front of him, "That's fine. If its okay… this bottle is on the down-hill side of half gone…will it be alright if I just take it with me?"

"What?...oh, yea, fine. Tell ya what Pete, give me a few minutes...when you're ready, come on back and we'll go downstairs. It'll be time for the poker game to get started a'for long."

Pete stood in front of the second floor office window and lightly parted the curtains with one finger. He watched the lamplighter reach out from his ladder to make a flame dance. His mind was busy with thoughts of how to skip town with Claypool's watch dogs sniffing every move he and Slats made. He thought they might have to split up, but if trouble was to come barkin' two guns would be better than one, and Slats' gun was the more experienced in recent times.

Keeping the relationship secret had been easy. There was no resemblance in their appearances. Pete was of sturdy build and red headed; compared with the tall, skinny frame of his dark-haired cousin they had no family likeness. The only outward tie was the Irish names and that wasn't anything a man could hang a hat on. The side-show antics they displayed at the poker table had left Claypool convinced the Irish cousins were nothing more to one another than poker and business acquaintances.

Slats was making his way over to *The Royal* for a few hands of poker, as was typical for any evening. He and Pete had announced tonight's game when they left the bank following their transaction with Carlton Claypool. Usual patterns would be the strategy the cousins would exhibit to throw Claypool's men off.

Slat's slow walk along the boards halted abruptly. He lifted the cigar from his mouth and squinted. He stood in quiet conjecture as he watched the young couple gallop up the street in the subdued evening light. *'That's Jimmy and Lilly…what the hell… they came back here!' 'Looks like they're heading toward the dancehall where they spend their time spoonin'.* The lanky Irishman chewed at his cigar, mulling the situation another minute or two before deciding he'd best go on to *The Royal. 'That boy's been a pain in my backside ever since we rode into town'.*

Linda Russell told him just a while ago that her hooligans didn't know – at least she made it clear that his participation in the rousting of the couple wasn't known. If Jimmy showed up, he'd handle it…quiet like for now, but the young outlaw had about stretched his luck as far as he was going to. *'I'll deal with that woman in a way she'll never forget if this causes trouble'.*

The slender man's mind was heavy with thoughts of getting out of Globe. He'd seen men cutting their eyes at him as he walked the boards, no doubt Claypool's thugs. That had been expected. He also had his brain engaged in thoughts of getting into the bank where fifty thousand cash dollars sat in a black valise – fifty thousand he and Pete should have in their hands – not in the bank.

Jimmy virtually flew through the batwings of *The Gem*. The blonde-haired outlaw snatched a revolver from the side of the first man he walked up behind. When the man grabbed at him as he plunged toward Ms Russell's private door, Jimmy slammed the gun up against the man's head and he sank to the floor like a sack of flour dropped from a table top.

Jimmy grasped the door knob and shook. It was bolted. He pounded the door with the gun butt. In short order a slot splintered through and exposed a sliver of light. He awkwardly brushed his wild hair aside, stooped and attempted to peek through the opening.

Saloon patrons hustled away, some out the swinging doors; others, with more curiosity and less fear, sought shelter behind tables and support posts as he screamed and pounded the door.

The bartender, always loyal to Ms Russell, stepped around the bar and was just a few feet behind Jimmy. He stood with his feet wide and solidly braced, holding a short-barreled scatter gun leveled at the boy's back., "What the hell you doin', boy?" he bellowed.

Jimmy jerked around, "Somebody's got to answer to me." He saw the bartender cock back both hammers – his eyes dropped, along with the high-pitched temper.

"Drop that there gun, Jimmy…I'll shoot you dead here and now – do it!"

Jimmy wiped angry tears from his face with the back of his hand. "Me and Lilly was drugged and carted out of town a couple of nights ago," he pointed the gun toward Linda Russell's door, "and she was the one that slipped us knock-out powder…I've seen her do that to people before."

"Boy, you can't go pullin a gun like you're gonna shoot somebody, especially a woman." His voice was stern and the shotgun enforced his standpoint. "You best drop that gun you're holdin'…don't make me kill you, boy!"

Jimmy melted apathetically. With low drawn eyes near tears, he looked at the shotgun under a tassel of hair. His tense lips relaxed. After a long minute of silence throughout the saloon, the hand bracing the pistol fell to his side and his arm hung limp.

Lilly had been standing back, her hands tucked over her mouth and tears welled up. She rushed to Jimmy and grasped his face in her hands, "Oh, Jimmy, you just can't do harm to Ms Russell…she's been almost like a mother to me."

Jimmy's expression withered. He gauged the girl's sobs and frustration, "Okay, Lilly, but somebody owes us. By

all rights, by-damn it, somebody's gonna answer to me."
He dropped the gun to the floor and kicked it toward the
barkeep.

He pushed scraggly, blond tresses of hair from his face
and stood in silence.

Lilly had retreated. She was standing behind the bar
with three of the other dance girls. They were all laden with
tears and embraced in a tangle of feminine anguish, looking
back at Jimmy and sniffing like school girls.

The exasperated young man had been notched down
and embarrassed.

He stuck his hands in his pockets. He fingered the roll
of cash and his mind flashed with a renewed ration of anger
as he conjured up the memory of Slats the day they arrived
in Globe and Slats refused to hand over his full share from
the bank robbery, *'Slats was in on this; ain't nobody gives a
man money and has him lifted out of town...unless it's money
owed...I'll deal with that bastard'.*

Lilly," he yelled.

She looked up amid sobs, her hands clinging to her
cheeks.

"Look at me, damn it," his voice was gruff and broken;
"I've got to go and find Slats."

"No!" She shrieked, "Not now, Jimmy...don't do it."

"You go on up to your room, I'll be back in not more
than an hour." He stormed out, pushing his way through.

The bar-keep edged back behind the counter-top, "Drinks on the house, men." He cut his eyes to the huddle of dance girls, "Girls, get over here and let these fellas enjoy yer company."

He knew Ms Russell had been in that private room where Jimmy had banged a crack in the door. He also knew she'd likely made her way out the back when the idiot youngster had tried to bust down the door. He'd check on her later.

- -

Slats McClary looked over the doors and pushed inside *The Royal.* He tilted his hat to a couple of the ladies who regularly toted drinks to the poker tables, "Evening, ladies." He walked over to his regular spot and adjusted his long body into the creaky chair.

"Good evening, Mr. McClary," Slats heard from a distance behind him. In the shadow, sitting at a table shielded from the main-room, he made out that it was Carlton Claypool, with two of his henchmen.

Slats forced a grin, "Good evening;" it wasn't the type of grin he'd use when pleased to be surprised. He thumbed his hat, then turned back toward his table, pulled at the looped gold chain and lifted his time piece knowing it close to the time he and Cousin Pete were to meet for poker.

And there he was…Irish Pete. He and Rink Slater, owner of *The Royal* were descending the stairway, sharing a light conversation.

As circumstance would have it, or experienced lawman's luck, Hank Darcy had chosen this evening to inspect *The Royal*. He entered the saloon three or four minutes after Slats. He stood near the door with his arms folded and his back against the wall.

He peered through the smoke-haze and his eye caught sight of a tall man sitting alone as the man snapped his watch open. He focused on him. *'Looks like the same man I saw once before'.*

Hank watched as Slats shuffled cards and seemed to be watching two men coming down the stairway. One of them was the bulky redheaded gentleman the tall man walked with a couple of days ago.

Hank's mind raced but he didn't move. His dark eyes went back and forth from the men on the staircase to the gangly man shuffling cards.

Suddenly the bat-wing doors flew open and a knurl-haired young man burst through like he might have been going to yell *"fire"*.

It was Jimmy.

He stood not more than ten feet from Hank; his shoulders hunched, his faced stoned up and he licked his lips. Hank had seen the look many times...there wasn't a doubt...the man was there to start a fight!

Jimmy charged forward, his direction set as he elbowed past a knot of miners, heading toward the tall man alone at the card table.

CHAPTER TWENTY-SEVEN – JIMMY DOSS, OUTLAW

Slats was unaware that Jimmy had entered the saloon. He lit a cigar and blew the smoke out of the side of his mouth and watched the staircase. The two men he eyed settled on the bottom stair and gazed across the large room filled with sounds of baroque men and feminine giggles, all buoyed by fallacious piano music.

"SLATS." The word broke above all else. A shush fell across the saloon as Jimmy pushed through the final steps. He stood over Slats, his voice like a preacher decrying the wages of sin being damnation, "Why did you do that to me?" The words were quick, filled with hate.

Slats said nothing. He looked up at Jimmy, shook his head side to side, reached over to the chair at his right, pushed it back from the table and nodded for Jimmy to sit.

Jimmy gritted his teeth. His angry eyes flicked, catching glimpses of the hushed stares of patrons. He disliked being so conspicuous. Uneasiness took him and his manner subsided. He sulked and remembered the time on the trail when Slats stood over him, gun in hand; and he remembered Slats' brutal killing of the Indian woman…and the man in Silver City.

Slats' fiery eyes enforced his implication. Jimmy could tell that sitting, as he'd been visually instructed, was the thing for him to do. He sank onto the chair, quiet but grudgingly.

The tall, skinny outlaw was calm, the fire in him unapparent to most beyond an arm's reach. He started in a low, explicit voice, "Boy, you've got the worst timing in the world!" He leaned over and said in a manner that Jimmy realized was absolute, "If you want to live through the night, shut the hell up…don't say another word. Just get your bee-hind up outta that chair easy-like," he looked square into Jimmy's eyes, "and get yourself over to that hotel room of ours, and stay there till I come for you later."

It was plain that there was more to Slats' warning than the simple response he'd demanded. The threat was sincere enough that Jimmy felt a shiver down his spine. And his thoughts turned to Lilly…he didn't want to die…he'd found a reason to live for the first time in his life. He glanced around like he'd just been told there was a rattler under his chair and if he was to move too fast he'd be poison-snake bit. He sat a few seconds longer before rising slow-like and walking over to a spot he commonly occupied when he watched Slats play poker.

Hank Darcy knew now! When he heard the name Slats; these two, the blond youngster and the tall, skeletal man were the two he was after, the outlaws responsible for killing Josh. His hand rubbed at the handle of the Colt, his thoughts were clouded with anger. He drew his teeth together and his dark eyes glistened. But he couldn't do it here – not now! Hank swallowed the lump in his throat and brought his mind back in order. He'd just have to hang on, he'd do what had to be done…for now, he'd settle back… he'd wait and watch.

Once Jimmy vacated the table where Slats sat, Claypool ambled over and stood for a moment. He looked down at the lanky card-shark, he clinched the lapels of his high-dollar coat and in a cold, coy voice said, "Playing again tonight, Kendrick…or is it Slats?" His tone dripped with ridicule.

"Tonight ain't much different than any other night. How about you, Mr. Claypool, you playing? I'd sure like to take some more of your money." His comment held personal amusement; he thought about the fifty thousand dollars.

Hank Darcy saw the exchange of looks and words between the stylish, self-centered card player and the fastidious wealthy-looking middle-aged man dressed in a gray striped coat and pants that had stepped out of shadows. He didn't know what to make of it. They seemed to be familiar with each other, but their mannerisms weren't of friendly nature. He brushed it off as a simple passing between two not-real-friendly acquaintances.

From the foot of the stairway, Rink Slater departed from the big Irishman and sauntered toward the bar. He'd noticed, along with everyone nearby, the kid with the lit fuse that affronted Kendrick McClary…and McClary blew out his fuse with not much more than a short whiff. He also noticed, along with Pete, Carlton Claypool left the saloon alone, his two henchmen remaining at the table in the dark corner.

Irish Pete stuck his big hands in his trouser pockets and upon arriving at Slats' table, withdrew his right hand and extended it, "Good evening, Mr. McClary, you ready to play some poker?" The hand shake was the norm; they always did it prior to dealing the cards. Pete sat down while lighting a fat, well-chewed cigar…as usual.

Slats shuffled the deck a couple of times, laid the cards aside, turned his head to Claypool's men and said, "You fellas play?"

They gave him a look of disgust.

Irish Pete rose from his chair, stood in place, scanned the smoke-filled room, and loudly appealed, "Anybody want to play some friendly poker…say a five dollar limit game?"

A pair of men dressed like traveling drummers, along with a man who looked the part of a slip-shod miner who'd had a few good days waved and walked from the bar over to where Pete and Slats were. They took chairs and initiated introductions.

Jimmy Doss made his way past Hank and out the door. Having witnessed the brief encounter Jimmy had with Slats, Hank knew the boy was a follower. The skinny man was a hardened bad man, likely he was the killer. Hank sauntered over to the bar and ordered a beer. He stood with his elbow planted against the bar, sipped his beer and studied the lanky man known as Slats. Now that he'd identified his targets, he needed to form a plan.

The poker game was lousy for the Irishmen; stakes were small and the cards were inhospitable. The usual humor Slats provided fell short, and the loud, boisterous laughter Cousin Pete Murray invariably manifested night after night, was absent. They had other things on their minds besides poker.

At five minutes past eleven o'clock Slats flipped an unworthy hand to the center of the table, rose, folded a few dollars and stuffed them into a vest pocket, "Gentlemen, my lack of luck has been your good fortune; enjoy it until we meet again!" He tipped his hat and turned toward the door.

Hank took a final swallow from a lukewarm mug of beer as Slats cleared the swinging doors. He fingered the Colt at his side as he set after Slats...but his path was interrupted by one of the Claypool men. The man inadvertently crashed into Hank and detained him but appeared to pay no attention to the ex-lawman. His interest was totally focused on Slats.

Hank backed off momentarily. He'd observed the two men who'd sat idly in the shadowed area but only now did he comprehend their purpose. Darcy hung back for a moment and then fell in behind the men who shadowed the fancy-dressed card-shark.

The long stride of the slender outlaw was vigorous. The pace hardly slackened when he took occasional looks over his shoulder. He was on a hard line toward his hotel room.

Hank kept his distance. The man in front of him, who followed Slats, didn't seem to care if he was being observed by the tall, skinny man. The man actually appeared to desire that his stalking after Slats wasn't to be secretive.

Hank watched the Claypool man push into the hotel lobby within seconds after Slats. He affronted the desk where a short, round-faced man with a lonely lock of long, black hair hanging down over an ear stood guardian. When the clerk offered a smile and voiced assistance, the surly follower from *The Royal* ignored him, grasped the guest register, twisted it around and drew a finger down the column, stopped, looked up the stairway and lipped the words, '*McClary, number twelve.*' Having assessed the whereabouts of his prey with a lengthy stare up the stairway, he moved to an upholstered chair and slumped down in it like a contemptuous coon hound that had treed a prey but awaited the pack.

'*Well this adds a chunk of rotten meat to the stewpot,*' Hank pondered inwardly as he watched the antics through the multi-paned front window of the hotel. '*No doubt Slats McClary knew the man followed him*'.

Hank needed time to foster a plan. He wanted both of the men he sought to somehow come together when the time – and place, were suitable for his intentions.

For now, he didn't know where Jimmy had gone; the boy was secondary in his thoughts, however, after he'd witnessed the personality traits of the two back at *The Royal*, the boy didn't have the sand to be the killer, but he was an accomplice and that meant he'd have to pay, along with Slats McClary.

Hank Darcy wouldn't rush; there was a right way to handle this, no need for hasty mistakes. To miscalculate might create undue hardship on his family back in New Mexico Territory. He could possibly be prosecuted on charges of murder and hanged if he botched this.

He knew the thing to do was go back to his room, gather thoughts, and work on details. The man that followed Slats to the hotel was set for whatever stay was necessary; he evidently was watching the tall outlaw under someone else's orders, it wasn't personal for him, just a duty he'd been assigned. That thought hung in Hank's head more like a winter coat hangs on a rack during the hot weather...it was there but didn't have real meaning.

The mountain air had cooled and a soft breeze provided a little comfort from the warmth of the early autumn afternoon. A few hours sleep for tonight would serve him well – just was planning would. He'd do both.

CHAPTER TWENTY-EIGHT – JIMMY DOSS, OUTLAW

The window of the room Slats shared with his youthful partner was open. A scanty puff of air brushed at the curtain. Young Jimmy Doss was spread out on the bed like the straw in a horse stall. The escapades he and his lady, Lillian, had endured had evidently worn on him. He spewed snoring that sounded like a carpenter rasping concaved barrel staves out of oak planks.

The gangly man scraped a chair under him; he straddled it, sitting backward with his long arms crossed atop the ladder-back and his chin resting on his forearms. He set his eyes on Jimmy and absorbed himself in thought. He sat that way for a half-hour, hardly moving any part of his body. He then rose and went to the open window. Sounds from the saloons were still in the night air. That would last until about two o'clock and stillness would then be in order for about three hours, an hour before sunrise.

He pushed the chair aside, deciding he needed to sleep for awhile. He lifted a blanket from the end of the bed and wrapped it around his shoulders. He then withdrew the satchel, which he'd packed earlier, from beneath the bed, lowered his lean frame to the floor and sat upright, his back against the door and the satchel drawn snugly beside him. He tilted his chin to his chest and closed his eyes.

The half moon floated through intervals of skimpy clouds for four hours and sat well above the mountain range to the west. The night air shushed the high-desert town of Globe as Slats and Jimmy slept.

It was time. Slats peered out the window before lowering a match to the wick of an oil lamp he'd placed on the floor behind the bed, away from the window. He placed a hand on Jimmy's shoulder and nudged it. He nudged him again. The disheveled young outlaw's eyes flashed open – they blinked, and he rolled his head, facing Slats standing over him.

"Wake up, boy."

"What the hell you want, *partner?*" Jimmy made the word sound empty and contemptible.

"Well, a couple of things – things you need to know, including how I'm gonna make you a rich man."

"Yea, I found out how you figure on takin' care of me, *partner*", he said it again, scornful and loaded with disrespect.

"Boy, I didn't have nothin' to do with whatever happened to you – whatever the hell you tried to accuse me of." Slats gnashed his teeth together and narrowed his eyes, "That Russell woman told me you and that gal-friend of yours was runnin' off together." His words were affable and convincing.

"She told you that?" Jimmy sat up, his eyes searched for honesty in the tall outlaw's expression.

"Damn right she did." Slats took a step, snatched a bottle of whiskey from the dresser top, pulled the cork and handed the bottle to Jimmy. "Maybe you need to take a drink and get yer mind straightened." Slats put his hands on his hips and leaned over, "Why would I want you to leave?" He shook his head like he'd done many times before when he'd implied Jimmy was seeing things the wrong way, "You and I are partners…real partners…a team!"

Jimmy's eyes widened, he took a swallow of whiskey, grimaced, and thinking about the roll of bills in his pocket said, "So what about the money?" He drew a mass of folded and crumpled cash from his pocket. He held it for inspection by Slats.

"Yea, I gave Ms Russell the money – that's your share, remember – that's what I kept for you so's you'd not spend it all. She said you and Lilly was leaving town – that you'd decided to marry up, and she asked me what I thought about that. Well I told her I was holding some cash you'd given me to hold for you, and I wanted her to take it to you before you left town – that's all." He punished Jimmy with his expression, and commenced to shaking his head again.

Slats' antics worked. "Take another drink, partner. You and me got some puttin' back to do." Slats took the whiskey when Jimmy lowered it from his lips, "Here, I need a drink of that too…kinda like a celebration for being back together."

The skinny Irishman wiped the back of his hand across his mouth and handed the bottle back to the gnarly, blond-headed boy he'd just twisted into a knot with his trumped-up story. The Doss boy scratched at his cheek and manufactured a slight grin, a grin of ridicule and embarrassment.

Slats pushed Jimmy's mind a bit further, "It's likely that Russell woman…maybe her and your gal friend together… who knows what a couple of females might cook up…and for whatever reason, made a fool outta you."

Several minutes and several drinks later, Slats pulled a chair to the bedside. It would be sun-up in a little over an hour and the plans he'd made – some while the poker game was taking place, and others after he found Jimmy in the hotel room had to be initiated. And there were other plans… the ones he and Pete had jointly contrived in the middle of the night following the fiasco that Claypool, his lawyer, and the banker, Bradley, had pulled on the Irish cousins. That was before the rich mine owner that they scammed could put his hounds in place to stifle any tricks they might pull, like leaving town with *his* mine-purchase money.

The liquid courage Slats had put into Jimmy was taking hold. Now was the time to move, getting that fifty thousand dollars out of Bradley's bank had to be done before daylight… and before it was time to meet up with Cousin Pete. He moved his chair square in front of the youngster who was sitting on the edge of the bed, still in stocking feet, but well on his way to being pie-eyed drunk, "Partner, you and me, just us two together, we're gonna make a withdrawal from the bank…fifty thousand dollars worth!"

"Whoa!" Jimmy's mouth froze in the oval of the word. "That's a lot of money…where'd you get money like that?"

"I didn't say I had it; I said we're gonna get it!" Slats put a hand on the boy's shoulder and nudged him up from the bed. "Get you boots on."

As Jimmy slipped into his boots, Slats buckled on both Russian, pearl handled revolvers. He slapped at both sides, apprising himself that the guns were in place, bent and picked up the satchel. He took his youthful partner by the arm.

Inside of five minutes the two outlaws had quietly slipped out the second floor door in back of the hotel, quietly made their way down the staircase and around the corner of the building…all without being seen, in spite of Jimmy's wooziness.

They arrived at the bank a half hour before sun-up and silently made their way to the rear of the bank building. A light shown through a small glass panel beside the door and a man sat just inside. "Hadn't counted on that," Slats whispered, more to himself than to Jimmy, who was close enough behind to hear. A few seconds passed with the two of them peering through the darkness.

Jimmy smacked his lips, "Don't look good, partner." Jimmy whispered.

"Naw, don't say that. This could be just what we needed," Slats whipped back quietly, "having him in there is as good as having our own key." He turned, bent and spoke softly, "Here's what we're gonna do…you," he pointed a finger in Jimmy's face, "are going to scrape like this," he placed two fingers on the boy's chest and scratched slowly, "on the door frame, way down low, like you was a dog. Keep low so's he can't see you," the tall oulaw hunkered down to emphasize. "And when that fella's curiosity gets the best of him he'll open the door." Slats nodded in appreciation of his idea. "That's when I'll reach in and yank him outta there and bash his brains in."

Jimmy broke a smile, and with whiskey-stench-breath, puffed a pint-sized laugh, "I ain't never been a dog before."

"And you ain't never been as rich as you're going to be tonight neither," Slats muttered back. "Now get over to that door – I'm right behind you."

The tassel-haired boy got down on all fours and crawled the short distance, lowered himself snug to the threshold and scratched…he scratched again…and again. Soon, just as Slats had drawn it out, the man inside the bank made his way to the door, held his ear to it and listened blinky-eyed. He flipped open both latches of the door and slowly opened it to the cool outside air. He extended his head, and just as planned, Slats yanked the man by the collar and smashed the barrel of a Russian.44 into the middle of his forehead. Blood spurted and the fellow quietly folded like a wet rag. They heaved him inside.

The minimal light inside the bank confounded undertakings. Slats located and turned a chair to face the back door they'd entered. He pointed to it, "Sit there, boy," he put a forefinger to his lips, "be quiet and keep your eyes open." He examined his cohort's eyes; although they weren't clear, he appeared to be stable. "And if anyone comes to the door – or within thirty feet or so, you let me know…but quietly!" With that Slats made his way toward the walk-in vault.

He scratched a match into flame. A brief examination and twisting of dials and he'd decided. He'd affix the six sticks of dynamite between the shiny wheel and the combination lock.

He returned to where he'd sat Jimmy and retrieved the brown satchel that he'd placed behind the chair. It held the blasting sticks. Jimmy looked at Slats and at the travel bag, "What's that?"

"Boy, "he said softly, "that's two things…the dynamite I need to blow open the safe, and the bag I need to tote fifty thousand dollars out of this here bank."

"What? You got dynamite?" His mouth hung open like a cave entrance.

"Yep, dynamite."

"You'll blow us to kingdom-come!" Jimmy's voice raised a couple of levels.

"No I won't…but I'll blow that vault door off." Slats dug a hand into the bag and lifted out the half dozen sticks of dynamite which were banded together.

"Holy, Jesus, Slats, you're going to get us killed." The words came from Jimmy as a plea.

"Wrong again, partner," he blew the word *partner* out of his mouth – a reminder. "I'm going to make us rich – not dead. Now get under that desk…and you might want to stick your fingers in your ears."

CHAPTER TWENTY-NINE –
JIMMY DOSS, OUTLAW

The dynamite did what Slats said it would. The vault door lurched open. The air filled with a black, rancid cloud littered with chards of paper, chunks of mortar and heavy dust. Slats scratched another match and lit a lamp. He waved an arm trying to clear the way and within seconds he located the black valise that Claypool had instructed the banker to put in his vault for safe keeping. He opened it. The money was still inside. He had to be quick; he grabbed up the case and placed it under an arm; located the valise he'd brought along and quickly found Jimmy.

"Come on, boy." Slats grabbed Jimmy by the arm and helped him shuffle out from under the desk and pushed him toward the vault. He stumbled forward. As the bewildered young man, who had become a bank robber and wanted for murder back in New Mexico Territory, walked a weaving path, nearly incoherent, Slats shouted, "Jimmy!"

When Jimmy turned and squinted through the dark haze with bleary eyes, Slats pulled a revolver from his waist band and shot him square in the middle of the chest.

Jimmy crumbled. With bewildered, misty eyes that begged compassion, he murmured, "Why, Slats?" He fell and rolled onto his back. His eyes glistened momentarily, and the empty stare was locked in place. Dark, murky blood oozed from his mouth and nose. A final waft of air blew through his teeth…he was dead.

"Sorry, boy…but I just couldn't leave you to be my damnation – you wasn't never gonna learn." He positioned the revolver on the floor beside the boy's body.

Slats jerked the bank guard's pistol from its holster, pointed the muzzle into the man's gut and fired; he then placed it in the guard's hand, folding three fingers around the inlaid pearl grip.

Slats made a hurried final assessment amidst the murky fog, kicked through fragments of rubble, shook his head in approval and made his way through the bank's back door.

The gray haze of pre-dawn and purple inauguration of a new day rose on the horizon as Slats raced down the back alley. Irish Pete was to have four fresh horses ready. They would meet behind the saddle shop and now with two hundred and eighty thousand in hand they'd soon be shut of Globe, and Claypool.

The plan concocted by the two cousins called for Pete to slip through the passage from his office, into *The Royal* and out a window that was well concealed by a grape arbor Rink Slater tended for the purpose of a token quantity of special wine once a year. The horses had been gathered by one of Rink's go-boys the previous evening, saddled and waiting.

Lamps were being lit; windows showing life sign, and doors were pushed open by curious town folks who'd heard the blast.

The long-legged Irishman had his legs pumping and his breath came in noisy bursts. He'd figured it would take less than two minutes for him to run the distance to where Pete was waiting, but he'd not considered the extra weight. It was going to take longer than he'd planned.

Confusion and turmoil would provide at least three or four minutes, and the cover of early morning light was with him. This was not the time to worry, the game had been set in motion and there was no stopping; all the cards were dealt – the ones peeled from the bottom of the deck were well planned!

Slats rounded the corner. He saw the big man on one of the horses and fashioned an exuberant smile of satisfaction. The fifty thousand from the bank was going to be news to Cousin Pete. Slats had schemed the morning bank heist of his own personal accord without Pete's endorsement or opinion.

Slats knew when Jimmy showed up after the arrangement hatched by him and Linda Russell, he couldn't allow the boy to live. And he couldn't dump the thought of leaving the fifty thousand behind…so the bank robbery, accompanied by Jimmy's death, was contrived last night in the hotel room.

The man standing guard at Bradley's bank opened another opportunity. Slats made it look like Jimmy had gained entrance to the bank by way-laying the guard with a blow to his head. It was set up to appear that Jimmy and the guard shot each other after Jimmy had blown the door off and readied to enter the safe; the gunshots were exchanged and they killed each other. It was made to look like the robbery had failed – no money taken.

To top it off, the explosion would provide cover for the Irish cousins, giving them time to vamoose out of town while the town busied itself with the explosion. Hopefully it wouldn't be discovered until later that Claypool's satchel with the money was missing from the vault. The plan was remarkable! The pieces went together like a child's picture puzzle, simple and snug.

Slats was almost there. The haze of morning begged the inception of better vision by the minute. Suddenly, he realized the man on the horse wasn't Pete after all! Slats hand dropped to his side and locked on one of the .44's.

Armed men emerged from out of nowhere. "Throw your hands in the air – now!" One of them bellowed. Hammers cocked in unison like a firing squad. Dark figures jostled closer in near mayhem, long guns and pistols flailing, all pointing at Slats.

In reflex, Slats yanked a revolver and fired at one of the dark shapes. A mix of red and gold lightning belched from the muzzle...and was answered by four rapid red-orange blossoms back at the thin, stand-alone figure.

Slats was hit. He twisted and went down.

A bevy of men jumped through the gun smoke. Rifle barrels held by two of them poked at the long-legged figure that squirmed in the dusty back alley.

A stout figured man with brass-rim glasses and a moustache stood over the skinny card shark. It was Marshal Karl Houghton. With him were four newly acquired deputies, all Claypool men...and all with guns still pointed at Slats. The gangly man moaned and tucked his right arm against his body – blood oozed between his fingers.

"That's him," one of the deputies drawled, "he's the one that came to the bank with Irish Pete when Mr. Claypool bought the mine from him."

"Damn shame we didn't kill him," one of the men mused.

"Mr. Claypool didn't want 'em killed. I reckon he's got somethin' in mind…maybe hangin' where he can watch."

"Just like the boss figured," Marshal Houghton nodded, "the two of them was workin' together."

Slats rolled onto his back and cradled his arm to his chest. He looked at the gathering of men and twisted his head around. He couldn't get an eye on Cousin Pete. *'Where is he?'*

The top of the sun edged over the horizon as two of the henchmen lifted Slats to his feet. "Damn, he is tall, ain't he!" one remarked.

The marshal opened the black valise, "Yep, like the boss said, these sons-a-bitches was trying to get outta town with his money. The both of 'em have cases filled with money. He's gonna be right proud of us, boys…maybe give us a bonus."

"Emmitt, you get on over to Claypool's place and let him know we got the two double-dealers for him, and we'll hold 'em here for a spell so's he can see the shenanigans they was workin'."

"What if he ain't up yet?"

Houghton answered, "Don't worry 'bout that… everybody's up – with that explosion and all down at the bank…now git ta goin'."

Pete was pulled out of the door of the saddle shop feet first. He was still groggy from the blow to his head, hands and feet tied with a rope that looped around his neck. The large leather case he'd toted stood open beside him.

"Boy howdy, if these two don't make a prize in a cake-walk," one of the deputies scoffed." He poked the barrel of his rifle into the cushy belly of Pete Murray and the big man stirred, shook his head, and looked around as best he could from the predicament he was in. The man then turned his attention to Slats, who was being bound, hands and feet, in the same manner as his onerous cousin. "That one there might be skinny enough to slip through them bars of that jail of your, Houghton." A nauseous cackle rose and faded from the provisional group of lawmen.

Slats was placed on the ground next to his cousin. Pete remained stretched out on the ground, still securely tied, but he'd fully regained consciousness. The two exchanged despondent glances – both obviously in pain and ripe with anguish. Their appearances ridiculed in comparison to the usual fine attire and proud demeanor they exhibited at a poker table.

Pete struggled to a position looking at Slats as best he could muster. Laying on his side and blowing dust as he spoke, he said, "What the hell you thinkin', cousin…you go off on your own like that! That fifty thousand," he clinched his teeth and spat, "is gonna get us killed." This was my call – my game, my rules." He spat at Slats.

"Bullshit," Slats barked back. "You had yourself all wrapped up like a Christmas present before I ever went to that bank…don't give me yer what-fors. If you'd done a better job of getting' here and having them horses set, we'd got out of town…with the extra fifty thousand."

"Shut up, you two," Houghton screamed at the Irish cousins, "neither of you was gonna get away from me…I had the both of ya pegged and in my sights for the past two days and nights. You featherbrained card-hounds ain't neither as smart as you think you are."

Town-folks gathered and milled about in the next quarter hour…as did Hank Darcy. He had gone to the site of the explosion first, the same as others. There, he'd witnessed the dead body of Jimmy Doss. He then moved on when he was made aware that the two Irishmen had been captured in the alley behind the saddle shop.

Men continued to gather, gawking at what the flashy twosome had faded into. Small talk among the onlookers varied – some faces showed tinges of satisfaction, but still others held token remorse. It was a meaningful, mixed, reflection of the regular saloon patrons and poker players.

Several minutes passed before the wealthy, fancy-dressed boss man was ushered to the scene in his usual well-appointed rig pulled by a pair of matching carthorses.

Hank stood among the crowd, watching and listening. This was Carlton's party; one might even say the rich gentleman reveled in it, handling it like he might handle a celebration, a chance to show off his wisdom and power.

CHAPTER THIRTY –
JIMMY DOSS, OUTLAW

Claypool shouted orders. "Get them over to your jail, Karl. We'll hold them there today." He scratched at his chin, "I'll decide how to handle the justice for these two-bit thieves after I get my money back in the safe in my office. I'll come up with something that any claim-jumper in the territory that might have an eye on my holdings will remember for the rest of their life."

"You want we should put 'em in a carriage – or on a horse?"

"NO,' shouted Claypool…make 'em walk." He leaned in closer to Houghton, "Don't you mess this up, Karl, or you just might be joining these two," he leaned back and glared at the man, "if you know what I mean."

Hank Darcy stood close enough to make out Claypool's instruction to Marshal Houghton. His emotions flexed. He still intended to make sure Slats McClary was to die. He judged that Claypool likely was of the same conviction, but he didn't say it – not where Hank could hear.

"Take them ropes off their legs so's they can walk." The marshal ordered, "But put a loop around each one's neck so we can tote 'em along. And I want a strong man on the walkin' end of them ropes. If either of these scallywags gets loose, there'll be hell-to-pay by the lot of ya."

The ex-Ranger followed along with the large group of men that fell in behind the deputies and their prisoners. At the front of the strange entourage was Marshal Houghton. A pair of deputies a short distance behind the marshal flanked the prisoners. The two biggest deputies each had a six foot length of rope wound around an arm; one end tied around Pete's neck, the other to Slats'. Another pair of deputies carrying shotguns brought up the rear.

Movement of the formation was cumbersome. The prisoners shuffled along in the dust, scornful and defiant of the indignity forced on them, especially in front of men where they'd always portrayed themselves as superior.

Anger still welled up in Pete. His Irish temper wouldn't let go. He kicked at Slats. When he did, it earned him a smack from the barrel of a ten gauge scattergun across his knee by one of the Claypool lawmen. He went to the ground cursing the man who'd struck him, and crudely promised the man he'd someday be sorry he'd done it.

Slats scoffed and ridiculed the big red-head, "You never was one to know when you're bested...even as a kid, you sissy-kicked when somebody stood up to ya."

"Shut up!" A deputy gave Slats a jab to his injured arm that hurt like blazes. He recoiled and tried not to react...he blinked and blew through gritted teeth.

Normal town activity was nullified, seemingly for the day. The Irish cousins and the regiment that forced them along held the town's full attention. The alluring peaks that silhouetted against the blue sky and the warmth of the early sun in their faces went unnoticed. All focus was on the dowdy pace of the assemblage of men that trekked eastward, toward the jail. Lengthy shadows of the loose organization of drably dressed men floated along in co-existence in the dust of the main street of Globe. Conversations were questions.

"Who robbed the bank?"

"What did the poker player and Irish Pete do?"

"What's gonna happen to 'em?"

Hank Darcy kept his eyes on the rake-handle, thin man who killed his brother. His mind shut out the majority of the low-spirited conversations taking place around him. He'd seen the emptiness in the minds of crowds like this before and had never been able to find that type of looseness in himself. It had always eluded him. Negligence of duty or avoiding responsibility had never been conceivable in Hank's life. Kate was aware of that segment of Hank's personality too. They had jointly acknowledged and talked about it. That was one of the reasons he'd left law enforcement, to see if he could at least reduce the constant feeling it dogged him with.

But it wasn't to be. He had to serve his convictions – he was instinctively required to fulfill his duty – as a lawman and in his personal life.

Right now he was close enough to carry out the justice that had engulfed him ever since he and Matt had constructed Josh's coffin. That was almost three weeks ago. But to carry out the role he demanded of himself wasn't possible. He'd have to wait. His family would suffer humiliation and go through hard times if he was to shoot his brother's killer here and now.

Without warning, a cloud of blood exploded from Slats' back. His body jumped in wild contortions. His head and arms jerked as he flailed into a twisted heap ten feet behind where his last step had taken him. A repulsive sound, a combination of a delirious yelp and voided wind spewed from his body. Slats' life ended in a hideous manner equal to the brutality he'd disgracefully inflicted on others for years. The wickedness harbored inside the man had sarcastically taken him as a victim.

Irish Pete folded – he flattened onto his gut in panic, afraid to move. He feared for his life. He was motionless for several seconds, every muscles tensed. His breath came in short gasps, sensing every inch of his body, figuring he was to catch a bullet.

It didn't happen.

When he realized there wasn't going to be more shooting, he rolled to look at Slats. Slats' mouth flushed with blood and a big hole bored through his chest. Pete cursed at him in both sympathy and anger, "Damn you, cousin, why the hell couldn't you leave well enough alone…why'd you have to take time to rob that damned bank?" Waves of red hair flopped down his forehead into his eyes. Anger within the big Irishman trumped the family attachment.

The deputies dropped to their bellies, except the one that held the rope looped around Slats' neck – he ran!

Marshal Houghton stood rigid. At first he seemed unaffected by the sudden chaos. But the man was petrified, unable to react. He was several feet in front of the assortment of terrified deputies and town-folks, his eyes blinked over his glasses as he flopped to his knees and looked back. He thought about Claypool!

Many of the followers, miners, clerks, and roustabouts ran to the cover of buildings aligning the street. Others stood numbed, watching in uncertain disbelief of what they saw.

JIMMY DOSS · OUTLAW

"Anybody see where that shot came from?" a deputy shouted as he ran to the front and stood next to the marshal who was still down. He scanned the crowd for an answer.

All eyes searched the distance before them, where the boom of the shot resonated.

"Down there...by the livery." A man shouted and pointed, "That's where. I saw the smoke to the right side of the barn."

"Yea, I saw it too."

Another yelled back, "That's over two hundred and fifty yards...you sure?"

Hank quickly made his way to Slats' body. An orifice outline with burned smudges that a man's thumb would fit into was in the center of his chest. Hank flipped him over. The exit crater in his back was the size of a saucer. Fragments of his heart, interlaced with slivers of breastbone fanned from the wound like flower petals in crimson mush.

Two of Claypool's men that had been deputized for the capture, bolted toward the spot the man claimed to have seen a puff of smoke.

Hank followed.

The two deputies worked the sides of the street, randomly seeking cover as they moved toward the livery barn.

Hank halted.

The deputies stopped and stood erect.

Don Russell

A boy with dark hair and not more than four feet tall, dressed in rawhide clothes and moccasins walked out of the double doors of the barn and started up the street toward the commotion. The gathering of townsfolk all stood quiet, their heads cocked and eyes fixed on him. He advanced as if he was surprised to see so many people gathered in the street.

A Claypool deputy shouted to him, "Boy, you seen anybody with a rifle?"

The youngster turned his head side to side as if he was looking for someone, "Nope...but I did see a man in a brown shirt – he wasn't carrin' nothin' but his hat...he went off that-a-way." The boy pointed toward the north where the creek ran under a timber-fashioned bridge.

"You ain't seen nobody with a rifle?"

The boy shook his head, "Nope" and then added, "I've gotta go find my pa, he's still in the hotel up town." He continued to walk up the street. His jade-green eyes were slightly moist as he glanced back over his shoulder at Hank Darcy. He never gave a hint of recognition.

Neither did Hank...but a warm, snippet smile crossed Hank's lips.

Crows gathered in the trees near the creek's bank.

The following day Hank Darcy sat astride his big black horse in front of the marshal's office. A hangman's scaffold was being built.

Two simple wood crafted caskets stood erect on the plank boards in front of the marshal's office, one of them noticeably longer than the other. The lifeless form of a tall, angular man slumped inside. A hand-lettered sign was pinned to his chest; "Kendrick McClary, Bank Robber And Killer".

The other casket held the body of a young man with tangled blond hair, his arms crossed in front of him. A sign identified him; "Jimmy Doss, Outlaw".